CU00867409

Cult of Death

Cult of Death

The Standard Book 3

John Reinhard Dizon

Dedicated to my dear friend Regina and her Dad Chuck —
semper fi.

Chapter One

Jack Gawain woke up that morning and stared moodily out the window of his loft apartment on Prince Street in the Soho area of Lower Manhattan. He was in a black mood, feeling as if he had hit a nadir in his life though there was no real reason for it. Most men would probably envy someone in his position. He looked across the bed at the sleeping woman beside him and knew that most men would pay a king's ransom for one night with her. He considered all the money they had in the bank, and the fact they had all the time in the world to spend it.

'That was the root of the problem. He had become an adrenaline junkie. There was sufficient action back in East Belfast around the turn of the century, but his arrest and incarceration at Maghaberry Prison brought it to an end. Since his pardon, he was trying to gorge himself on life as if every moment as a free man could be his last. Now that he had decided to go into retirement, the thrill was gone and the life of leisure had become ennui.

"You up already?" she yawned in her bewitching Corsican accent. She turned to face him, her china-blue eyes tugging at his heartstrings as she peeked through the veil of raven-black hair across her face. He had dozens of affairs in his life, but if he had ever fallen in love this had to be it.

"Aye. What d'ye feel like doin' today?"

"Do you think we can not have an agenda today?" she brushed her hair away from her face with an ivory-skinned hand. "I would really like to take it easy today."

"Of course, love," he smiled, scooting over alongside her.

"Oh, no, I'm exhausted," she rolled onto her back. "Where do you get all your energy from?"

"Nay, I was just lookin' fer a kiss," he insisted, leaning over and smooching her full red lips. "Why don't I run downstairs and get us some breakfast?"

"What's going to happen when the stock market crashes? One of us will have to learn to cook."

"I'm not too shabby around th' kitchen when push comes t'shove. Plus, ye can't tell me yer th' only Frenchwoman on earth who doesn't know how t'cook."

"So buy groceries, let's see who can do better."

"I've got all I want right here," he grabbed her ankle and kissed her toes.

"You've had quite enough for now," she pulled her leg away, sitting up in bed. "Besides, I know how it works. You'll grow used to me, and soon you'll be out looking for a change."

"Are ye mad, woman?" he chuckled, rolling out of bed. "No red-blooded man in his right mind could ever have enough of you."

"Do you really have to parade naked in front of the window?"

"Do ye figure someone with binoculars is havin' a peek? It's you they'd be lookin' fer, don't ye know?"

"Why don't you just draw the shades?" she reached over and grabbed her robe off a chair.

"'An' should I block the sun on such a gorgeous day as this, love?" he gazed out the window at the busy Soho streets below. "Ye should really enjoy life, stop an' smell th' roses."

"You don't just smell the roses, you devour them," she padded in her bare feet across the carpet.

"Pretty soon there'll be no roses left in your life."

"Well, I'll still have you, won't I?" he came over and hugged her, her generous bosom pressed against his barrel chest.

"Of course, *mon cher*," she kissed his lips. "Now run along. I have to take a shower. Perhaps if you behave we can cuddle up this afternoon."

"I'm not sure I can wait that long," he stepped back, showing her how his manhood had been stimulated.

"Oh!" she pushed his hands away as she headed for the bath-room. "Take that thing with you."

He chortled as he headed to his closet on the far side of the spacious bedroom, picking out a black workout suit. He picked out a pair of black briefs and socks from his drawer, inspecting himself in the mirror as he dressed. There was a Gold's Gym not far from the loft, and he stopped in three times a week to keep his powerlifting physique build in good order. He kept his dark hair cropped short and cut a handsome figure, for which he was thankful considering the life of debauchery they were leading. She was not much of a drinker, and he was always careful not to get tipsy and become unaware of his surroundings. Still, there were calories to be considered, and so far neither of them were the worse for wear.

"Why don't you take a shower before you go out?" she called from the adjoining room. "I'll leave it running for you."

"Nay, if I go in there with you freshly scrubbed, most likely I won't let ye out."

She shut the door firmly, causing him to chuckle as he shov-eled his keys and his wallet into his pockets. He put on his $10,000 Rolex and his $5,000 diamond ring, then started to pick up his ankle holster but thought better of it. New York had one of the toughest gun laws in the States, and having someone spot it in a careless moment could prove costly. He never left home without it when dressed in his street clothes, but workout suits weren't quite as concealing. He shoved the Glock-17 to the rear of the drawer and headed for the door.

Just as he reached for the doorknob there was a knock. He looked through the peephole and saw a young black man outside.

"Aye, what d'ye want?"

"Jack Gain? I have certified mail for you. I'll need your signature."

His nerves began twitching as he thought of going back to get his gun. Only this was a high-rent loft building and it was highly likely that he had slipped past one of the other tenants at the door to deliver his letter. The question was: who could have known he was here? MI6, most likely. Why send a letter? To keep from having an emissary hurt or killed, he figured. Or maybe it was Shanahan. There was only one way to find out.

"Slip it under the door, then."

He heard the crunching of paper at the bottom of the doorway.

"Sorry, sir. It won't fit."

"What th' bloody hell," he growled. "Hold on, then."

He went back to the bedroom and pulled open the dresser drawer, pulling his Glock out of its holster and stuffing it in his jacket pocket.

"What's wrong?" Lucretia asked, having emerged from the bathroom in her robe, toweling her sopping wet mane.

"Some silly bastard with a certified letter."

"Who knows you're here?" she was startled.

"We're gonna find out," he replied, heading for the door and pulling it open.

At once he was hit with a Taser, the electrical weapon causing an immediate neuromuscular incapacitation. He lost control of his muscles and dropped to the tiled floor, his body spasming as he was nauseated by a wave of vertigo. He was dragged from the doorway as two men raced into the apartment, a third man rolling him over and handcuffing his wrists behind his back. He started to struggle but could feel a hypodermic needle plunge into his neck before he passed out.

Five hours before on the other side of the Atlantic Ocean, William Shanahan sat in the living room of his townhouse in London, mulling over his recent decision. His marriage to his beloved Morgana had not been the honeymoon in paradise he had envisioned. Over the past six months, they both found that the wife of a Secret Service agent was not without its difficulties. Despite the fact that he had finally got the desk job at 85 Albert Embankment he had dreamed of, he was still being called out for emergency meetings at odd hours. He was the liaison with the British Foreign Office on Middle Eastern affairs, and the situation in Iraq and Syria was making life ever more hectic.

His gorgeous wife's intellectual capacity made it all the more arduous. She made it a point to find out everything she could about Middle Eastern affairs to be able to discuss things with him. At times it seemed as if she knew more about it than he did. He saw politics as a necessary evil and could care less as to which sect or faction in the Middle East was planning to destroy each other. He so much wanted to leave his work at the office, but as soon as they had time to sit around and talk, it was always back to the same droll subjects.

What made it all the more disturbing was the fact that he could not talk about the nature of what he did or where he had to go when he was called out after dinner. The calls came at least twice a week, and one came after they had already gone to bed. It was the cardinal rule of espionage: you never told a loved one what you did lest they became a bearer of secrets that could make them a target. Yet true love made one jealous, and she resented the fact that she had no way to confirm whether he was going out on business or pleasure. She trusted him in every way, but she didn't really know him deep down. His job would not permit it. And that bothered her more than anything.

"Good morning, dear," he greeted her as she emerged from the bedroom on the way to the kitchen.

"You're up early," she said briskly, pouring water for coffee. "I suppose you've made a decision."

"I've thought it over carefully," he cleared his throat. "I don't see how I can turn them down."

"That's just fine," she dropped the glass pot loudly into the coffee maker. "I suppose I can get my job back at the airline while you're gone."

"Oh, come now, Morgana," he stared at her as she briskly yanked cooking utensils from the cupboards. "We've plenty of money, there's no reason for you to go back to work."

"And what am I supposed to do, sit around here and get ulcers, worrying if you're coming back home in a body bag? I thought that was over for us, William."

"Darling, you're not looking at the big picture," he got out of his armchair and came over to her. She was a Nicole Kidman lookalike with long blonde hair, emerald eyes, and an hourglass figure that never ceased to make his blood percolate. "You've been watching the BBC, you know what's going on more than most of the people at Vauxhall Cross. ISIS[1] is threatening to divide Syria and Iraq, and turn the mid-region into an Islamic caliphate. The public's laughing about it, but the Foreign Ministry is watching the Iraqi government collapse day by day."

"Spare me all your corporate bullshit," Morgana blazed at him. "What are you gonna do, pull on your Superman costume and save the world? All by yourself? The fate of the United Kingdom depends on William Shanahan, is that it?"

"It's not like that. You know I was there last year, I got inside an Iranian facility. I've got the experience, the hands-on contact. I also served in Iraq, I know the Shiite people. They need someone who can lead an undercover team. Lives are going to

---

1. Islamic State of Iraq and ash Sham

be at risk. How could we live with knowing people got killed over there when I could've been there to save them?"

"And suppose you can't save them? Suppose you're killed? You asked me to spend the rest of our lives together, to give you my hand in marriage, and now it comes to this? This is a dirty trick, William. You told me we'd live the rest of our lives here in London until you retired from your desk job. Now you're going right back to where you started, risking your neck to get ahead. You're already ahead, I'm the one who's losing here. You're taking from me what I've already got, what I thought I would always have."

"Morgana, you know I love you more than anything in this world," he took her in his arms. "There is nothing that's worth risking our marriage for. If you really don't want me to go, I won't. All I ask is that you reconsider the situation before you make your decision. The Chief of SIS[2] and the Foreign Secretary both mentioned my name, as did Mark O'Shaughnessy. But I'm not going to risk losing you."

"What about the baby? We said we were going to try and have a baby by the holidays."

"Of course we will. There's nothing else I would want more."

"Oh my gosh," she pulled away and stood with her back turned in the corner. "You have no idea what things are like in America after that war. Our soldiers are coming back with post-traumatic stress disorders, crippled and disfigured, with all kinds of problems. Suppose something happened to you over there? Suppose our child had to live with that while they were growing up?"

"It's not going to happen, my love. You know who I am, you know what I'm capable of."

"That's the James Bond secret agent who you told me about after we started dating. That's not the William Shanahan I mar-

---

2. Secret Intelligence Service

ried. I remember the guy I had to stitch up after he nearly got killed on a golf course in Miami Beach. You said that'd never happen again."

"All right, darling," he came up and put his arms around her waist. "I'm not going if you don't want me to. All I ask is that you think about it. But I won't go if you don't want me to."

"I keep thinking about Jack," she put her hands over his. "You're not holding anything back from me, are you? You wanted that desk job more than anything else. Are they leveraging you into taking the assignment?"

"Of course not, precious," he hugged her tight. "You know Gawain was always full of bluster. That night when we ran into them at the restaurant, he may have been just bragging. Lucretia was a EUROPOL agent. It makes no sense whatsoever that she could have been the Black Queen of the Citadel. The entire Citadel Gang was shipped off to Guantanamo. Any one of them could have gotten a pass by identifying her as the Black Queen. Not one of the twelve men said a word. Plus, how could have she been out in public going out to restaurants with him when all of Europe was looking for the Black Queen? The whole notion is ludicrous."

"You told me she disappeared from EUROPOL. Why would've she walked off a job just like that? Especially after you said she was wounded."

"You know Jack," he put his face in her hair and breathed her fragrance. "He's got a way with women. Look how he got on with your friend Fianna, not to mention that girl from Florida, Darcy Callahan. He went AWOL on us as well. Mark O'Shaughnessy's still looking for him, but it's just for debriefing. It's quickly becoming past history, just tying up loose ends. MI6 could care less about Jack and Lucretia. If they thought Lucretia was the Black Queen, there'd be a worldwide manhunt for them. It's simply not being done, sweetheart."

"You've already washed enough blood off these hands, William," she turned around and took his large right hand in hers.

"I promise you," he kissed her forehead. "I won't go unless you let me."

And so it was that William Shanahan attended the meeting with Colonel Mark O'Shaughnessy at Vauxhall Cross that morning. He was resolute that he would make no decision without Morgana's consent. He was an Acting Deputy in the Middle East Department under Director Eric Young, who was also in attendance. There was also a strikingly beautiful young woman who he had never seen before. He was fairly certain that this was going to be the briefing for the upcoming mission. It was going to be extremely difficult to explain to Mark that he might have to back out of the operation. It might even result in losing his position in the Department, but he realized his marriage was more important. Morgana had become that precious to him.

"Captain Shanahan, this is Lieutenant Jessica Anderson," Mark made the introduction. "She served with the Special Forces Support Group in Iraq and Afghanistan. She's a new addition to the Middle East Department and has been assigned to the Director's current project."

"A pleasure to meet you."

"Likewise," she gave him a firm handshake. Jessica stood 5'7" and weighed 140 pounds, with auburn hair, hazel eyes and a slight tan that William perceived came from a salon. She had an hourglass figure and a generous bosom that would make her useless on the field in the misogynistic Middle Eastern society.

"As you both know," Mark opened the meeting, "the situation in Iraq has grown increasingly volatile over the past few months. ISIL has occupied the border regions between Syria and Western Iraq, and ISIS is in virtual control of Northern Iraq. Our American allies are the only thing that's keeping Baghdad from being overrun. The Iranians are surging across the border into

Eastern Iraq by means of clandestine operations, and the Syrians are conducting their own raids into Iraq on their border. The Foreign Ministry has no intention of deploying troops, but we know full well that if the Americans are drawn into a full-scale war, we'll be sucked in right behind them."

"Our major concern is their capture of abandoned Iraqi chemical weapons factories in Northern Iraq. Most of the plants were certified by UN inspectors to have been rendered inoperable. That hardly means that they can't be put back together again with the millions of dollars being donated to their cause by Sunni billionaires throughout the region," Young spoke up.

"So you'll need a team to go in and make sure ISIS can't finish anything they may have started."

"Captain Shanahan has a unique talent for cutting to the chase that I'm sure the Director is familiar with," Mark explained to Jessica after a short pause. "Of course, the situation is a tad more complicated than it may seems, so permit me to go over the mundane details."

"My apologies, sir, I didn't mean…"

"I'm certain you did not, Captain," Mark said coolly. "Nonetheless, we would not want to pass along any classified information concerning this operation without feeling confident that you are absolutely clear as to what will be required."

"Most certainly, sir."

"Very well. Your mission will be to move into the Sunni areas from Baghdad, posing as converts to Islam who wish to participate in the *jihad*. You will then make your way into ISIS territory and locate the key figures in the enemy infrastructure. Your objective is to locate any and all chemical arsenals in ISIS' possession and take steps to assure their destruction."

"So we're going to search the ntire Iraqi desert and blow up the ISIS chemical arsenal," William mused. "Do you think there might be time for some sightseeing in Tehran?"

"If you will allow me," Eric grew testy. "As you are well aware, the Israelis have a major stake in the outcome. All of the participants in this conflict share a mutual desire to annihilate the State of Israel. We have contacted both the Americans and the Israelis. We have the assurances of the CIA and the Mossad that we will have their full cooperation. Two of the Israelis' top agents will be in contact with you in Baghdad. They will be working with you to complete this mission. Your team will have full access to both the CIA and Mossad's network, as well as the air and artillery support of the United States Army."

"If I may, sir," William spoke up. "The Muslims hold women in almost as low esteem as they do Jews. Suppose things were to go sideways out there at any point. I could find myself working alone if they were to sequester Lieutenant Anderson and liquidate the Israelis."

"This is a joint operation, Captain," Mark pointed out. "You're working alongside the Israelis, not with them. If they are taken off the field you would follow standard procedure. The Lieutenant's job is to manipulate the segregation to her advantage. The female population is considered inferior and non-threatening. The situation will provide its own cover."

"Any questions, Lieutenant? Captain?"

"Not at this time, sir."

"Colonel, may I have a word?"

"Certainly. Dismissed, Lieutenant. Thank you, Mr. Director."

"I hope this has nothing to do with a sightseeing tour of Tehran," the 6'4", 300-pound Colonel leaned back in his seat once the door closed.

"No sir, although it is somewhat of an unusual request."

"Pray tell."

"I'm going to need you to call my wife to get her permission for me to go."

Jack Gawain woke up and found himself in a darkened room resembling a police interrogation room. He was incensed that he had been apprehended after being subjected to such drastic measures. Even more vexing was the act that Lucretia had just gotten out of the shower and might have been wet or naked if she was tasered. He was handcuffed and fitted with restraining straps and ankle locks, and obviously they had anticipated him coming out of his stupor by now.

"So were ye silly bastards watching me sleep?"

"Ready to talk?" the man across the metal table asked.

"Where's Luci?"

"She's talking to somebody else."

"Well, who the feck are you and where am I?"

"You're at the Metropolitan Correctional Center. I'm Bob Probert with the CIA. We could step aside and let the DA's Office deliver an indictment for unauthorized possession of automatic weapons. Of course, they'd probably turn you over to the FBI, who would have to give you up to Homeland Security. They would nail you for aiding and abetting, and Lucretia Carcosa could end up in Guantanamo on suspicion of being the Black Queen of the Citadel."

"Real tug o' war ye've got goin' here, mate," Jack lounged back in his chair. "Obviously ye think I've somethin' t' offer, or ye wouldn't be here blowin' smoke up my arse."

"The problem you've got is that you're not MI6, you're an operative. That's about a half step above what the UDA[3] used to call a supergrass[4]," the husky agent leaning in the corner behind Probert spoke up. "We let MI6 know you're here as a courtesy. They may make an attempt to get you back for debriefing over Operation Citadel, but Carcosa's gonna fall right through the cracks."

_____

3. Ulster Defense Association
4. informant

"Aye, so what's yer offer?"

"We want you and Carcosa to come to work for us. We've already painted the broad strokes for MI6, we'll be filling in the fine lines should you accept the deal," Probert replied. "They already got all the intel they needed about the Citadel from your ex-partner, William Shanahan. They're willing to wait to debrief you on what you know about Carcosa. Our mutual interests in the so-called Islamic State make MI6 more than happy to oblige us."

"Ye mean that jackpot they're playin' fer over there in Iraq? That's an army the Sunnis put together, it's not a terrorist group anymore. At least that's how th' BBC puts it. Besides, they don't like Christians an' they don't like women on either side. I don't see how we'll be of any use."

"We'll be the judge of that," the second agent said. "The whole planet has videos of your girlfriend threatening the US and NATO with a dirty bomb attack. She asked for a ransom of one billion dollars. You were the one who blocked her attempt at the Eiffel Tower. After that you disappeared along with her at her hideout in the Carcassonne. That's where we recovered a Soviet-made nuclear warhead. I don't see where either of you have a choice here."

"Talk is cheap, fellow. We saw the tapes. I don't think that Black Queen looks much like Luci at all. Plus, as ye say, I'm the lad who saved th' Eiffel Tower. I should be a national hero in France right now."

"We'll see how far that flies when the French people find out you're been shacked up with Carcosa for the past few months," the agent retorted.

"I'm sure they'll appreciate me taste in women. An' let's not forget that she's a decorated EUROPOL agent. She may have gone AWOL, but it don't put ye anywhere near framin' her fer bein' the Black Queen."

"Wanna take that chance, Gawain? You know Guantanamo is our version of the Roach Motel. Roaches check in and they don't check out. When she goes in, we'll tell her you rolled to keep from having to go there yourself. She'll never have the opportunity to find out for herself. And it'll fairly well guarantee you'll never see her again to tell her your side."

"Well, ye got me by the balls, ye bastards, so squeeze away."

"We've got strong connections with the Peshmerga in Kurdistan," Probert revealed. "They're looking to establish an independent state, and that will necessitate them clearing their borders of ISIL extremists. We've launched a joint operation with the PUK[5] in conjunction with the forces under Colonel Armand Hussein of the Peshmerga. Our goal is to neutralize the threat of the Ayatollah Qom Diabolus, who represents the radical elite of the Islamic State."

"As you know, ISIL is funded by a large network of Sunni corporations who have contributed billions of dollars to the anti-Shiite cause. Diabolus has used some of the money to recruit mercenaries and assassins across the globe. His intent is to form an elite team of specialists whose mission will be to eliminate individuals and hard targets delaying the spread of the Islamic State across the Middle East," his partner revealed.

"Should you and Carcosa accept our offer, the two of you will be inserted into Kurdistan where you will hook up with Colonel Hussein's forces," Probert continued. "It will be your job to locate Diabolus' team and dispose of them by any means necessary."

"So you want us to hit the hit men. Just lovely."

"You've built a reputation for random acts of violence," the partner shot back. "You did quite a job in tearing up the Cuban Syndicate in Miami last summer. Not to mention taking down

5. Patriotic Union of Kurdistan

the Mafia and the Russian Spetsnaz a few months ago. Together with the Black Queen, you two should make a great team."

"Flattery will get you nowhere. Anyway, if I go along with this hash, when do I get to see Luci?"

"If your girlfriend decides to play ball, we'll put you together with Joe Bieber within the next twenty-four hours," Probert replied. "You remember Joe, he's been your main contact with MI6 on your last two missions."

"Aye, he's a standup fellow. Better that that bastard holdin' up th' wall behind ye."

"That Carcosa's got some crappy taste in men. Of course, considering what a skank she is, she's probably happy to take whatever she can get."

"I'll remember ye, fellow. Hopefully we'll meet again and discuss it at length."

"I'll be looking forward to it, you son of a bitch."

"Okay," Probert got up and knocked on the metal door. "We'll get you and the Queen cleaned up and ready to go, unless she has any objections. You'll be meeting with Bieber in a few hours, then your next stop will be Baghdad. Good luck."

Jack smirked at their backs as they exited the room. He was going to make someone pay dearly for this inconvenience, and he greatly hoped the CIA would be among those picking up the tab.

On the outskirts of Deir Hafer in the east of Aleppo Province in Syria, twelve men staggered across a finish line at the end of a hundred-yard stretch marked by twelve rows of ten event-class hurdles. Located near the Syrian Desert, the temperature hovered around one hundred ten degrees, and tempers were very short. These men were the last of an original group of one hundred and twenty. They had lasted ten weeks, and they were assured this was the last day of testing. Only they saw this as just another torture run, and more than a couple had reached the limit of tolerance.

"Damn raghead sombitch comes out here and gives us one more run, I'm gonna tear his head off before I leave here," the American gasped for air, his voice choked with desperate rage.

"Hang on, mate, we've reached the finish line," the Australian was bent over, trying to fill his lungs. "Look around ye, there's not a man here who can take much more. Hold on and we'll all go out together."

Almost as if on cue, they could hear the roar of an eighteen-wheeler as it came around from behind a craggy hillside. The truck pulled up and came to a halt about fifty yards from a huge cavern entrance hewn into the rockline.

"Come, my friends," the man known as Mustafa Hilal came forth from the cavern, becoming them forth as a second truck pulled up behind it. "Come to the truck, you have reached the end of your journey."

The twelve men trudged up to the truck as the driver and his assistant hopped out. They came around to the rear of the vehicle and threw it open to reveal a portable shower stall.

"Hah!" the Israeli stopped to assess the situation with arms akimbo. "So these fanatics decide against us and we get the gas? I don't think so."

"I'm willing to take the chance," the Frenchman scowled at him, walking up to the truck and pulling himself inside. "Better in there than out here."

The Frenchman was rewarded by the hiss of water as the shower heads gushed forth sprays of lukewarm water. He had to back up to the rear of the van as his teammates raced for the truck and lunged beneath the blessed cascades. Only the American lingered, pulling off his sneakers and socks before entering the truck.

"You will be their leader," Hilal came over to Mike Mc Cord.

"Yeah?" he squinted before climbing into the truck. "Well, don't that just make my day."

"Praise be to Allah," Hilal smiled as he patted Mc Cord on the shoulder and walked off.

"Allah *chingar*," the Texan muttered.

When the men emerged from the truck, they were directed to the second vehicle where a folding table was brought out along with ice chests, beer kegs, water and beverages. Fruit and sandwiches were also provided as the men ate ravenously. They were also provided with black robes, sandals and khalats to be donned before entering the cavern. The twelve men exchanged fist bumps and high fives, elated in knowing their ordeal had come to an end.

"I congratulate you, my brothers," Hilal addressed them as they took seats in a small room just inside the main entrance that was modified to serve as an enormous loading dock. "The US Navy SEALS and the British Special Air Service once prided themselves on having the toughest training programs known to man. Rest assured, you twelve men have far surpassed it."

"I can vouch for that," the crewcut Englishman spoke up.

"Each of you were carefully chosen, as were the one hundred and eight others who did not make it. The Ayatollah made it clear that Allah would select only those who were strong enough to stay the course. I am certain that we have been blessed by his choice. As agreed, each of you will have one hundred thousand US dollars transferred to your private Swiss bank accounts. After your briefing, you will be provided Internet access so you can confirm the transactions and make further arrangements as you desire. I would just avoid sending the money anywhere Homeland Security can get their hands on it."

Laughter eased the tension in the room.

"Three double-wide trailers are being brought into a horse-shoe canyon not far from here. You will be divided into four-man fire teams and will share each trailer. You will be in direct contact with commanders of the Islamic Army and coordinate activities with them as our march to victory continues. As of this moment, this elite squad will be known as the Hammer of Allah. You will be referred to in communiques as the Hammer. It will be a name that will strike terror in the hearts of our enemies in a very short time. Now, at this time I will ask that you follow me. The Ayatollah himself has come to give you the blessings of Allah."

The squad was caught off-guard by the revelation, and followed Hilal down a rocky corridor into a large chamber carved into the inner cavern. He stepped aside, pulling a large curtain back to permit entrance to the soldiers. They saw a floor of black marble which shone like glass before them, leading to a great dais upon which sat a golden throne. Upon this sat a black-robed, white-bearded figure that emanated an aura of pure evil. His demonic features were enhanced by the torchlight that flickered around the walls of the chamber. Ayatollah Qom Diabolus arose and walked to the edge of the platform to confront his visitors.

"What is this, a movie?" the Russian snickered.

"This ain't no fuckaround, dude," Mc Cord hissed. "You best get with the program."

They heard Hilal recite an arcane chant behind them, and they fell to their knees before bowing forward and banging their foreheads against the floor, extending their arms in supplication. They rose to their feet and stood at attention in squad formation as Diabolus spread his hands before them. His eyes rolled back in their sockets as he chanted an occult spell written before the dawn of man. The hair rose on the napes of their necks as they felt the temperature drop twenty degrees inside the room. At once, the dais was covered with a thick white smoke that belched from behind the throne. When it cleared, the Ayatollah had disappeared.

"Glory to Allah," Hilal whispered. "The mission has begun."

Chapter Two

Debbie Cantor unleashed seven thunderous roundhouse kicks against the heavy bag, creating the heavy indentation she sought before stepping back. She was pouring sweat and would probably lose five pounds this afternoon. Once she hydrated, she would put four pounds back on. If she starved herself, she would be a pound lighter tomorrow. It probably wouldn't happen, but it was the thought that counted.

"Do you really think you'll ever be able to use that stuff?" a familiar voice called from the rear of the darkened gym.

"Yeah, as a matter of fact, I do," she grabbed a towel off a dumbbell rack and wiped her face. "One day somebody's gonna come up behind you. Those fancy contraptions of yours won't do you a damned bit of good. And somebody'll have to get you out of it."

"You'd finally be returning the favor," Glenn Frantz walked in and took a seat in one of the comfortable armchairs she had set next to a coffee table and bookcase by a far wall in the basement gym.

"So you make a decision on the apartment?" Debbie began throwing light jabs at the bag.

"Shoshana loves it," he took off his gold-rimmed glasses and produced a handkerchief, cleaning his lenses before wiping his brow. "I'm gonna be popping ragheads for the rest of my life to pay it off. Eleven million shekels, can you believe it? Where do you get the *chutzpah* to ask for that kind of money?"

"Try looking at a penthouse on Rothschild Boulevard," she picked up her pace, throwing left-right combinations at the bag, bobbing and weaving as she did so. "Friend of mine is talking twenty million. He said they would consider him putting up his firstborn as a deposit."

"You have friends? When did that start?"

"Asshole."

"C'mon, take a break, you're making me sweat."

She came over and dropped back onto the armchair across from him. He refrained from making a crack at the sight of her generous breasts shifting with the impact. She was a beautiful woman with ivory skin, thick black hair that reached the middle of her back, and an hourglass figure enhanced by athletic musculature. She had light blue eyes, a longish nose and full red lips, with dimples that gave her a deceptively innocent look.

"So have we heard anything from Colonel Naphtali yet?"

"There were three targets they were looking at along the Gaza Strip. Only something else has come up. He was just about ready to call us in for a briefing. There's something big up ahead, but he wants us to sit tight until he gets word from the Director."

"I hope this doesn't have anything to do with that shit in Iraq," she rolled her eyes.

"Well, now that you mention it."

"Oh, come on, Glenn!" she tossed her towel onto the rubber-matted floor. "We've got tenure, we should have a say in this! I don't have a problem with getting even with those Hamas bastards. I don't see where they get off asking us to hop on a truck and ride out into the desert to get into some jihadist gang war. That's kid stuff. That's for rookies. We should be way past that."

"It's not that simple anymore," he leaned back in his chair. He resembled a college professor with shoulder–length hair, a thick mustache and a tennis player's build. "The Islamic Army's taken control of abandoned Iraqi chemical weapons plants recently. We have no way of knowing whether they can be restored to functionality. Plus there's rumors of mercenary units being recruited from around the world. Put two and two together, and they could eventually be sending elite squads to Western countries around the world with suitcase WMDs."

"And what, you and I'll be able to stop them?" she grew exasperated. "They're getting money from Sunnis around the world. That includes the Saudis and their billions in oil money. The Prime Minister needs to get everyone to back up and let us send our army in to take out the Islamic Army. People like you and me are about picking off insurgent leaders on our borders."

"Well, when you get elected Prime Minister, then maybe that's how it'll go down. Right now they think having a team dropped into Northern Iraq and taking out a key chemical depot will result in a serious setback for them."

"You already met with them," she stared at him.

"I had dinner with Captain Schneerson. He gave me the big picture but didn't tell me what we'd be taking out."

"You know, they tell you to jump and you ask how high. If we go in there, I'd get split up from you and have to walk around with a bag on my head. If they found out we were Jews they'd cut our heads off at the nearest bazaar. We're in our mid-thirties, for gosh sakes. How many jobs have we done for them, thirty-five?"

"Thirty-seven."

"Yeah, so you're counting. We've done our time, we deserve a say in where we go."

"We were on a short list. If we get picked, it'll be by the Prime Minister himself."

"Oh my gosh," she shook her head. "So when will they make a decision?"

"I hear they may finalize plans tonight. If so, you'll probably get a call in the morning."

"Just like that, huh?"

"I don't see you sitting out on Drummers Beach. You look like you just can't wait to get back out there."

"I'm not exactly looking forward to it, but I'll be damned if I'm not ready."

"Yeah, well," he got up from his armchair. "Better get home for dinner, the kids'll be out of school soon."

"Did Avi make the soccer team?"

"He's one of the finalists. You know you're not a Frantz if you don't always get put on the short list."

They walked up the steps to the grade floor of her two-story townhouse on Mifrats Shlomo Promenade, just a short distance from the Jaffa Port. The property had been owned by her grandmother and was bequeathed to her parents, who gave it to her as a graduation present. She had invested most of her earnings with the Mossad into remodeling the place. It turned out to be a wise decision considering the real estate prices in the neighborhood.

"This is bullshit, and you know it," she folded her arms as he unlocked his Kia Picanto. "They should be sending someone else."

"They have no one else, or they wouldn't be sending us," he said before they exchanged embraces. "There are some hard times ahead, they don't need martyrs. They need survivors."

"Yeah, so they can send us out again," she patted Glenn on the back as he slipped into the vehicle. "Give Shana and the kids a hug and kiss for me."

"I think Avi'd rather get it from you. He's got a crush, you know."

"Wait until he meets some of those cheerleaders with the soccer team."

Debbie Cantor and Glenn Frantz were children of Russian Jews who migrated to New York City after the fall of the Berlin Wall. Their parents were close friends who had relatives in Israel. They eventually became Zionists who realized their dream of living in the Promised Land, bringing their grade school children with them. Debbie and Glenn were raised as devout nationalists who embraced the principles of Zionism. They both enlisted in the Israeli Army and were recruited into the Sayeret Matkal special forces group. Upon leaving the military, they joined the Mossad and became part of an elite assassination unit. They sold their souls to the State of Israel, though Glenn had enough of his own left to raise a family and become a model husband.

All Debbie had was the Mossad.

Both her parents had asked her to retire on their deathbeds, and she made empty promises to each of them. She thought herself as a turtle, like the two she kept in her giant fish tank in her living room. She lived inside her armor and only came out when she was needed. If she removed her armor, the pain she would share with the hundreds of families torn by extremist violence would destroy her. She knew too many alcoholics in law enforcement and the military, and she was damned if she was going to become one of them.

She went into the refrigerator for a baggie filled with rabbit food, dropping some in for Cuff and Link. She switched on her wide-screen plasma TV before heading for the shower, preparing for another early bedtime. She would watch the newscasts before she went to bed, psyching herself up for the mission ahead. She only hoped she could choose her own time and place to die. She wanted to die in defense of her own country. She damned sure didn't want to die in some Arab desert where no one would know or care who she was or what she did. It was the least they could do for her in exchange for a lifetime of service…

…as short as that life might be.

William Shanahan and Jessica Anderson were polite yet reserved towards each other on the flight to Baghdad. They respected each other as people as well as their personal accomplishments. She knew he had been decorated twice by the Queen, and he knew she was one of the only women to fight with the SAS is Iraq and Afghanistan. Only it was their appearances that caused them to perceive weakness in each other. They thought of each other's movie star looks as liabilities, and made them doubt one another's ability to endure extreme pressure.

They were booked into Al Rasheed Hotel in downtown Baghdad, where they were allowed to unpack before being brought to an emergency meeting. Although the area near Al Zawra Park was considered an amber zone, restrictions was tight enough for a personal security detail to escort them from their hotel door to a military transport vehicle. They both changed to collared shirts and jeans in order to avoid suspicion by insurgents of being diplomats or military personnel. Yet they watched furtively out the windows for signs of suicide bombers as they made their way to the UK Embassy off the Qadisaya Expressway.

They were awaited by Assistant Director Robinson of the Foreign Office and MI6 Major Helmsley in a conference room on the first floor. There were dossiers set before two seats at the end of a long table, across from which sat the two executives.

"As you can see, we're trying to make this appear as innocuous as possible," Robinson opened the meeting. "With the situation being what it is, everyone stationed here has been instructed to keep in mind there are eyes and ears all around us. The politicians are sending this deal to hell in a hand basket. We can only hope that our agents can make a difference before it all goes to waste."

"The Yanks are talking about not putting boots back on the ground, yet they've got over a thousand so-called advisors here and plenty more to come," Helmsley growled. "You know they're just looking for a reason to bring us in behind them. This Foreign Minister will have them leading him in by the ring in his nose. All the bloody ragheads need do is fire a missile at one of their aircrafts and take out a couple hundred troops, and we're back to Square One. Our nation can't afford another war, you see. If we strike quick and strike hard while we've still time, perhaps we can avert a national disaster."

"So when will we be placed in contact with Colonel Hussein and his troops?" William asked.

"We'll be taking you out by helicopter after dark. You'll be escorted by three gunships to deter any ambush attempts by the insurgents. You've been given cover identities that will allow you to assimilate into the Kurdish community. Captain Shanahan will be traveling as Dagon Al Hillah, and Lieutenant Anderson will be acting as his wife Nadalia. You will be expected to observe all the customs and protocols of the native community. Colonel Hussein and his staff are the only ones who will know your true identities. Your lives will depend on guarding them jealously."

"As you know, the Kurds are caught between a rock and a hard place in this conflict," Robinson continued. "They are seeking autonomy although the government wants to make them part of a united Iraqi coalition. Both the Sunnis and the Shiites would love to have them on their side, and the recruitment efforts are hard and heavy. We are going to spread the word that you and your friends are dissatisfied and wish to join the Islamic State. Once you've made contact, we will expect you to infiltrate the ISIL forces and neutralize this man."

"This is Mustafa Hilal," Helmsley opened his folder and turned it towards the agents. "He is a top military advisor to Ayatollah Qom Diabolus. As you know, Diabolus recently fled from the UK to avoid prosecution for treason and acts of terrorism against the Crown. We suspect he will become the spiritual advisor of Abu Bakr al-Baghdadi. This is what Parliament believes will be the modern-day equivalent of Antichrist and the False Prophet. You can understand why the Director wants Hilal either abducted or eliminated."

"So we have a choice," Jessica smiled curtly.

"Not much, I'm afraid. The chances of smuggling him out of Northern Iraq are slim to none. Eliminating him should be a more realistic goal. Our concern is that the Ayatollah may be thinking of building his own elite army, equivalent to a Republican Guard. Logic would dictate that he would entrust this task to Hilal. If successful, this would provide Diabolus with a private army entirely independent of al-Baghdadi himself. Think of a radical elite army that could reach across the planet and strike any target Diabolus chooses. It could result in a worldwide catastrophe."

"How will taking out Hilal make a difference?" William asked.

"Apparently Hilal has developed a recruitment network that is allowing him to bring mercenaries and radical crusaders in from around the globe. He must have found a way to do so that is going undetected by the most sophisticated law enforcement agencies. We will infiltrate it if we can, but destroy it we must. Keep in mind that this is going to be seen as Hilal's intellectual property, so to speak. The only reason why is hasn't been placed at al-Baghdadi's disposal is because of the Ayatollah. This is a highly-protected individual, and it's all the more reason why he needs to be taken out."

"So, in essence, we're trying to get to a man that, theoretically, al-Baghdadi has not gotten to as yet," William mused.

"The key to our success is the Peshmerga," Robinson insisted. "If you remember your military history, there is a strong resemblance between the Kurds and the Montegnards of Vietnam. They are fearless mountain fighters who have endured decades of social injustice and persecution at the hands of the government. They were victims of chemical weapon attacks by Saddam Hussein. They fought alongside the Allies, but as soon as we left they were victimized once again by the Shiites. If we can make the Sunnis think they are willing to join forces against a common rival, well, there's our angle."

"Everyone knows Colonel Hussein's reputation as a fierce tribal leader," Helmsley pointed out. "He's fully willing to cooperate with us provided his position within the Kurdish nation is not compromised. In other words, he'll play ball up until the time he actually has to step up to the plate. He will never lead his people against the Iraqi government as long as the Kurds remain part of it. Part of your job will be to make ISIL think Hussein is unhappy and might defect."

"And he'll go along with this," Jessica frowned.

"As long as it keeps you alive and as long as he doesn't have to back it up."

"Well, I can't wait to meet him," William said. "He must be quite a fellow."

"He does make an impression," Robinson smiled. "That I can assure you."

Colonel Armand Hussein stood 6'2" and weighed 265 pounds of solid muscle. He had wrestled on the Iraqi Olympic team and was also a national powerlifting champion. His head was shaved and he wore a thick black mustache that made Jack Gawain think of an Iraqi version of Mr. Clean. Yet the man seethed with energy, his black eyes continually assessing his surroundings. He quickly evaluated the Europeans who had been brought to his command tent and realized they were people worthy of his mettle.

"So they have sent you here to kill the Ayatollah."

"Well, actually they told us we had t'take out his All-Star team. Of course, if we get that far, there'd be no point in not takin' him out for the hell of it."

"We were told you were sent to kill Diabolus," Hussein twirled his mustache. "You won't be able to accomplish one task without completing the other. Make no mistake, if we help you get inside and you kill his mercenaries, if you do not kill him we will send you back to finish the job."

"This is superfluous," Lucretia waved her hand. "Do you think if you send us in there, we would leave anyone alive?"

"I could imagine a situation where you would have to destroy your targets before fleeing for your life. Diabolus would have to be included among those targets."

"Whoever you leave behind can overtake you in flight and stab you in the back. We leave no one behind. Ever."

"I like this woman," Hussein broke into a grin. "I have a feeling she is willing to back up her words. We will get you as close as possible to Diabolus and his men. I am sure your government has sent you because that will be close enough."

"So how are we t' go about this? Yer not goin' t'point us in the general direction an' send us on our way, are ye?"

"Here is a map of the region," Hussein picked a map from a nearby table and spread it across the larger picnic table at which they sat. "As you can see, our territory overlaps numerous borders, including those of Syria, Iraq and Iran. Our sources are fairly certain that Diabolus and his forces are holed up in the mountain areas around Aleppo along the Syrian border. His advantage is that many of the tribes in the region have joined the rebellion against the Syrian regime. These forces have fought alongside ISIL and consider them allies. Our advantage is that Kurds will never fight against their own people. They may fight alongside the Sunni but will never take sides against their own brothers."

"Well, we're all the way over here outside Kirkuk. That's about five hundred miles from here. How in hell are we supposed to get t'Point B, then?"

"By convoy, of course. There's no way we could fly you there. Keep in mind you will be moving through ISIS-held territory. They will be suspicious of Europeans and curious as to why you are bringing a woman along with you. We cannot provide a constant escort as it could be tracked and perceived as a hostile force. You will have to proceed along a network of rendezvous points. Hopefully we can remain one step ahead of the terrorists and help you reach your destination."

"An' suppose things don't work out as planned?"

"You'll be captured and most likely killed."

"Well, I guess that takes care of that. Luci, you can stay here an' help tend to th' camp while I attend to this."

"I was going to suggest that you do the same," she replied curtly.

"Our contacts at MI6 made it clear that you were to be moved through the desert into Syria to deal with this problem. Both of you."

"So actually you've not a clue as to how this is goin' down, do ye?"

"On the contrary. We've got a plan, but we won't be able to set it in motion until sunrise. You will get some rest, and we will see how things go in the morning."

The platoon had roasted a couple of goats and prepared a cauldron of rice, giving the couple a platter along with bread and wine. The couple munched happily on the meal, ranking it alongside their supper at the Al Mansour Hotel for its delectable flavor. Lucretia considered it a far cry from anything she had ever eaten on the field while training with the Citadel. Once finished, they were given sleeping bags and pup tents that they pitched alongside the platoon tents as everyone retired for the evening.

Jack tossed and turned for the few hours the platoon was allowed to slumber. This was probably the worst deal he had ever gotten himself into. Even worse, he was being forced into it alongside the only women he ever loved. He didn't realize he loved Lucretia until the last couple of days. The anger and concern he felt when they were captured, and the emotion he felt having her out here with him was an epiphany for him. He never felt anything like this before, and all he knew was that he had to get her out of here in one piece. They had to get back to where they were, get back on with their lives. Only now he knew he had found the one he wanted to spend the rest of his life with.

He knew he was a fish out of water in this situation. Granted, he and William Shanahan managed to disarm a nuclear missile in Iran last year, but they were part of a commando unit that walked them into the target site. He had spent his entire career on the streets of Belfast, and had only left for that life-changing month last year during Operation Blackout. Miami Beach was a far cry from the Tigris River. If they got captured out here, even if they escaped, where the hell would they go? He had to wonder whether this was MI6's way of getting rid of them once and for all.

The sound of a truck arriving in the distance startled him, and he rolled out of his sleeping bag to realize how cold the desert had gotten. He saw Lucretia crouched alongside her own tent, glad to see that Jack was up as well. They watched as the perimeter guards signaled with flashlights before the truck continued past them and rolled to a halt outside Hussein's command tent.

"Okay, love?" he came over and stroked her face.

"Try not to display emotion," she gazed reassuringly into his eyes. "They may perceive it as weakness."

They watched as two men entered Hussein's tent. After a few minutes, a soldier came out of the tent and walked towards the couple, beckoning them forth.

"This is Aleem Al-Saleh," Hussein introduced them as they entered the tent. "He is the leader of the squad that will escort you across the border into Syria. He and his men are from a tribe that live along the Iranian border. They have lived alongside Shiites all their lives. They are Kurdish brothers, but they can pass as Shiites if necessary."

"Aye, well, I'll take yer word fer it," Jack and Lucretia exchanged handshakes with the slender militia fighter. "Th' sooner ye get us t'where we're headed, th' sooner we can get th' job done an' get back t' where we came from."

"Patience is the key here in the Middle East, my friend," Aleem assured them as they followed him back to the truck where his squad awaited. "Everything comes to those who wait. The one who moves first has often made his last move. Especially in war."

"Well, maybe we'll be able to teach each other a thing or two," Jack smiled, exchanging knowing glances with Lucretia as they climbed aboard.

Mike Mc Cord stared moodily out the window of the armored truck as it rumbled across a rickety bridge over the Euphrates River. He and the squad were heavily armed and given their first mission by Mustafa Hilal. It was the kind of mission that most of them had taken part in throughout their careers, which didn't make it any more palatable. The Islamic State was intent on consolidating their holdings along the Syrian border in Northern Iraq, and they would crush any resistance from either side. The residents in the area were used to playing politics as a means of survival, but Abu Bakr Al-Baghdadi would no longer tolerate the ambiguity.

Mc Cord had accepted this deal with mixed emotions. A hundred grand was not anything to turn his nose from, though there had to be a lot more where that came from if he was to stay in the game. He knew ISIL was being bankrolled by millionaires throughout the Middle East, so they wouldn't run out of money any time soon. If they played their cards right, they could all become rich beyond their wildest dreams. Only the radicals were going to have to be curbed eventually, and everywhere he looked there were nothing but radicals. The lunatics had overtaken the asylum, built an army and now declared themselves a State.

He remembered the veterans' stories about Vietnam, how the terrorists did the unthinkable in winning the war. Once Saigon fell, then Phnom Penh and Vientiane went next. That's how it could go here. First Baghdad, then Damascus, then...who knows? Wherever they went next, there would be billions of dollars in oil money awaiting. A gig like this might turn into some kind of retirement plan. If the Ayatollah turned them into some kind of Republican Guard, who knows. Mike Mc Cord might be a Minister of Defense one day. Fancy that.

That Ayatollah was a crazy old son of a bitch: that was a fact. He must have been some kind of magician back in the day. He had the whole cavern near Aleppo rigged with special effects. He made smoke and fire appear from nowhere, he could disappear at will. He even threw a lightning bolt or two. The only thing was, more than a couple of guys on the team spoke a number of Middle Eastern dialects, and between them they spoke over a couple dozen languages. Whatever the old man was praying about, it wasn't in any earthly language. That was for sure.

"Hey, that looks like it over there," Mahomet Qawi, the Iraqi commando riding shotgun, pointed to the village in the distance as they came over a ridge along the dirt road. He had been one of Saddam Hussein's elite Republican Guard back in the day. "Doesn't look like they have any militia force in the area."

It was a little no-name collection of shacks and tents outside the town of Mayer in Syria. The residents relied on nearby wells as their water source and traded at local bazaars with the townsfolk for their living. They depended on Mayer for law enforcement, and their neighbors were subject to the Aleppo Governorate in such matters. In most cases, the village elders settled disputes and would call a meeting when an issue was a concern to the whole community.

Mahmud Al-Bab was the oldest resident of the village, and he and his granddaughter were the first to see the truck as it rumbled towards the well at the center of the camp. He shuffled towards the vehicle as it came to a halt, the young girl clutching his arm in trepidation.

"Greetings, my friends," he called as Mc Cord hopped out of the vehicle, followed by Qawi and the rest of his men. "Have you come for fresh water? The marketplace hasn't opened yet."

"We do not come for refreshment of the body, but of the spirit," Qawi replied in Syriac. "We have come to spread the good news of the caliphate, and the establishment of the Islamic State. Have your people pledged allegiance to Abu Bakr Al-Baghdadi?"

"Come on, Grandfather, let us go," the girl was frightened.

"No one will hurt you, little girl, come here," Qawi beckoned. "Let us give you our blessing."

"Come on," the German grimaced. "Business before pleasure."

"Let him be," the Russian grunted. "The body can be used for psychological effect."

Mc Cord came forth and grabbed the old man by the arm, leading him toward the camp as Qawi dragged the weeping girl to the rear of the truck. The mercenaries followed their captain as he forced Mahmud over by the well.

"All right," Mc Cord spoke pidgin Syriac, firing his .357 Magnum into the air. "You get your people out here. We want to make sure everyone here is loyal to the cause."

The men and teenage boys of the camp came out to investigate as the women and children gathered fearfully at the thresholds of their homes. The ten soldiers pushed past the men and headed directly for the hovels, conducting random searches as the women protested in vain.

"We need to know that the people of this village support Abu Bakr Al-Baghdadi and the caliphate," Mc Cord holstered his weapon, draping his arm over Mahmud's shoulder. "The Islamic Army is moving through here in the name of Allah, and we want to know they will be greeted with open arms by the loyal Muslims of this community."

"Ho! What have we here!" yelled the Israeli named Judah, emerging from a miniature trailer. "Who lives in this shithole? Whose shirt is this?"

"I am Abbas," a middle-aged man stepped forth from the group of males by the well. "I served with the police in Mosul during the time of Saddam Hussein. After the war I returned here to live with my family."

"You are a Sunni?" Mc Cord demanded. "Then why are you living in the land of the Shiites? Why are you not home supporting your people?"

"The Shiites are everywhere," Abbas insisted. "They have taken over the Iraqi government. They are in power there just as they are here in Syria and over in Iran. No matter where we go we are oppressed."

"Then why are you keeping this rag as a souvenir?" Judah walked over and threw it in his face. "How do we know you were not with the Syrian police?"

"He is my grandfather," a young man stepped forth. "He speaks the truth."

"Are you from here?" Judah growled. "Are you a Shiite?"

"We are all Sunnis," a husky man stood beside his friend.

"This old bastard is trying to turn you against Abu Bakr Al-Baghdadi," Judah drew his pistol and pointed it at the old man's head. "If the Islamic Army came here and was forced to withdraw, he would put on that shirt and betray his faith."

"Stop pointing that gun at my grandfather!" the young man walked up, at which point Judah turned the weapon on him and shot him between the eyes. Abbas lunged at Judah and was dropped to the dirt with a crushing right.

"I am the imam at our place of worship," another elderly man came forth. "How can you execute Muslims without a trial without evidence of wrongdoing? Is it wrong to defend one's grandfather for being slandered in public?"

"He will set an example for those who rebel against the Islamic State," Mc Cord signaled his men towards Abbas' trailer. "Do you wish to join him?"

By now the women and children of the village were huddled at a distance from the well. Everyone cried out in protest as the soldiers joined together in shoving the trailer off the wooden beams that held it above the ground. There were loud crashes from within as the old man's belongings were tossed asunder. Abbas' home nearly broke in half as it landed with a great noise. The campers watched in horror as the beams supporting were hauled forth and thrown to the ground. The Nigerian produced a hammer and spikes as his comrades set the beams in the pattern of a cross.

"No! I beg you, in the name of Allah, don't do this!" Abbas' daughter raced towards Mc Cord.

"Shut up, you bitch!" Judah stepped forth and struck her to the ground, causing teeth to fly from her mouth.

Once the mercenaries built their cross, they ordered two men to dig a hole alongside the well. They next dragged Abbas over and nailed his wrists to the cross before lifting it up, dropping it into the hole. The old man cried out to Allah before fainting.

"He'd have better luck praying to my dick," the Salvadoran chuckled.

"Shut the hell up," Mc Cord hissed. "We're devout Muslims, remember?"

"This is what happens to anyone who betrays the Islamic State and the Caliph of the Muslims, Abu Bakr Al-Baghdadi!" Judah pointed to the old man, whose wrists poured blood down his arms onto the ground. "We are the Hammer of Allah, the avengers of the faith! We will purge all traitors and blasphemers who betray the one true faith! Get on your knees and beg forgiveness of Allah for having stood by and allowed iniquity to thrive in your village!"

Mc Cord chuckled as the entire community dropped to the ground, banging their foreheads against the dirt and stretching their arms out before them. They cried out to Allah for mercy as the soldiers returned to the truck. The Russian commando named Rusev shook his head as he saw Qawi already sitting in the passenger seat.

"What in hell!" the Australian named Dundee stared at the naked body of Mahmud's granddaughter. She was lying in a puddle of blood at a distance from the truck, her groin horribly mutilated.

"That is so the people cannot spread the word that she was raped," Rusev grunted as he climbed into the truck.

Once the squad was inside the vehicle, Mc Cord backed up and did a semi-circle to head back to the dirt road. As expected, the truck ran over the girl's midsection, causing her entrails to spurt out onto the desert sand. The people waited until the truck drove off before leaping to their feet and tending to the fallen. They pulled down the cross and pried the nails loose from Abbas' wrists while others carried the body of his grandson. Some tended to his daughter while others rushed to tend to the mangled corpse of Mahmud's granddaughter.

A group of young men rushed into town to notify the authorities of what had happened. The campers knew that their complaints would fall upon deaf ears. All of Syria was held in a grip of terror as the Islamic Army grew nigh.

Only Allah could stop them…

…yet they wondered whose side Allah was on.

Chapter Three

The platoon made its way along the rows of crucified men, twelve in all. The victims had been captured in the town of Akashat along the Syrian border. They were accused of being Syrian spies by the company of ISIL troops in the area. Over a thousand people attended the executions while the remainder of the population of five thousand remained in their homes. They watched and waited until the rebels left town, but had been warned not to take down the corpses until the following day.

They were greatly relieved when the platoon arrived shortly before dark.

"Looks like crucifixion's become the new fad around here," Debbie Cantor looked around before walking away from the spectacle. A number of residents gathered to take possession of the bodies. "I don't think they appreciate the irony."

The Iranian captain watched as Debbie made her way over to a group of townspeople to find out more information about the ISIL guerrillas. He derisively spat in the sand away to the side where Glenn Frantz stood.

"This is ridiculous," Malik Shiraz growled. "It is bad enough that we are conducting joint operations with infidels. To add insult to injury, we are working side by side with women."

"Look, we don't like the situation any more than you do, all right?" Glenn spoke excellent Persian. "We are soldiers just like you, we take orders and we carry them out. The Prime Minister is not prepared to put any more boots on the ground here. He has agreed to send advisors and that's all we are doing, advising. I suggest that if you have any issues with this, you take it up with the Ayatollah or whoever."

The Mossad had arranged for the agents to pose as MI6 operatives in a joint operation with an elite unit of Iran's Revolutionary Guard, the Quds Force. MI6 had agreed to work with the Mossad in a joint effort to locate and destroy any chemical weapons captured or developed by the Islamic Army. They were informed that there were two MI6 agents working with Kurdish troops in the area, but they would delay contact and make themselves known when the time was right. Glenn's only concern was the possibility that he and Debbie were exposed, which would result in them being executed on the spot.

"The only concern I have right now is finding the bastards who did this," Shiraz narrowed his eyes. "They are trying to destroy the Shiite communities throughout Iraq and Syria, but we will destroy them before they destroy us. Undoubtedly they will attempt to make their way to the highway and join with their forces outside Damascus. If we can overtake them and cut them off, we can annihilate them before they can reach safety."

"If we come directly at them through the desert, not only will we be in plain sight, but we could be moving up against reinforcements. I think we should move in a three-pronged attack formation. We will let Debbie lead the frontal advance so you and I can flank the insurgents once they're located."

"Are you suggesting I order my men to follow a woman into battle?"

"It is a smart move. She is excellent at taking evasive action. If they pursue her across the desert they will suffer losses. It will give our forces time to bracket the enemy and take them out with a pincer movement. If you put one of your men in charge they will move straight ahead when they come within striking distance. The ISIL units will reinforce and break the jaws of our trap."

"My men are well-trained in strategy and tactics. They do not need a woman to tell them what to do."

"Your men have no battlefield experience," Glenn said curtly. "Iran has been in no wars since the days of Saddam Hussein. Everyone knows the history of the SAS. This woman can lead your men to the jaws of hell and back."

"The SAS," Shiraz mused. "That could make a difference. How strange it is that the Jews would allow a woman to serve with the world's most fearsome special forces unit."

"Who are you calling Jews?" Glenn placed his hand on the butt of his holstered Glock.

"I, uh," he stammered. "Is it not well known that the UK's Ministry of Defense is run by Jews?"

"That is a pack of lies manufactured by your pathetic Propaganda Ministry. I demand an apology."

"We should not let our tempers get the better of us," Shiraz said evenly as a couple of his men looked over to see what was happening. "Perhaps I spoke out of turn."

"Very well. But make no mistake, you and your men will never again refer to either of us as Jews. Regardless of what our socialist press says, my Government has no love for Jews."

"Of course, my friend," Shiraz allowed himself a smile. "It is good to know that our people share that common ground."

Debbie was commiserating with the elderly women who had gathered near the crucifixion scene along with their daughters and grandchildren. They all told her stories of the Islamic Army having victimized their town time and again. They told her how ISIL had stolen their chickens, robbed their stores at gunpoint and abused their women. They blessed and praised her, never having seen a woman in arms before. They told her they hoped she would make a difference in speaking out for the women of their community.

"Do you know where the rebels are hiding?" she asked, having joined them in a far corner by a small fountain near the marketplace. "Do you see which direction they take when they come and go from the village?"

"They are obsessed with the phosphate plant and the uranium mine along the outskirts of town," a young girl revealed. "Ever since the Americans invaded our country, the mine was shut down and the plant closed. At first they only came to steal, kill and destroy. Now they send men inside the plant and the mine every time they come by. They have warned our people to stay away from those places. We know they pay informants to tell them if anyone dares trespass. Now both places are avoided like the plague."

"Are you women Sunnis?" Debbie asked.

"I am a Sunni, but my daughter's husband is a Shiite, and my granddaughter's father is a Kurd," the old woman replied. "We are not prejudiced here. We are simple people, trying to make a living and do the best we can. We are all good Muslims, we do not discriminate against one another the way those fanatics do."

"Can someone take me to the plant?" she asked.

"No one will go near the place until dark," a young woman spoke up. "There are too many informants who would betray others to the militants. If you wait until then, perhaps one of the young boys will take you."

"Let me speak with my partner. Do you have a booth here at the market?"

"We sell dates and figs over there near the corner," the old woman pointed to a rickety stand. "One of us is always there. If you come again we will talk."

Debbie returned to the company and pulled Glenn aside.

"The townspeople told me that the rebels have been seen around the abandoned phosphate factory and the uranium mine. If you can get Shiraz to camp out near here, I can get someone to bring me inside."

"Who do you think you are, Wonder Woman?" Glenn squinted. "If the terrorists are keeping watch over those places, they're probably planning to get them up and running. If you get caught snooping around there by yourself, they'll cut your head off."

"You can come out and cover me."

"You know better than that. If both of us leave camp, nothing'll stop Shiraz and his men from clearing out and leaving us stranded. I'll have to come up with a story to get him to set up surveillance at the al-Waleed border crossing. That should give you enough time to get in and out before he decides to cross over into Syria."

"That'll work," she agreed. "I'll be meeting my escort after dark."

And so it was that the Mossad agents prepared for one of the most perilous episodes in their careers.

William Shanahan and Jessica Anderson found Colonel Armand Hussein to be a man of action. He loaded his battalion on a convoy and headed across the desert towards the Syrian border. The plan was to encircle the eastern outskirts of the Iraqi city of Tal Afar. There was a strong possibility that the largely Sunni population would be sympathetic to the rebels. The Sunnis appreciated the Kurds' reputation of being fiercely independent. They would place their trust in the Kurds' neutrality and hope they were not as predatory as many of the warring factions.

"This always feels like running the gauntlet," Jessica said tautly, looking in all directions through the dusty windshield as William steered the armored car down the paved road. "I've lost count of all the vehicles we lost to landmines and roadside bombs."

"I always consider the odds," William tried to remain nonchalant. "There's around thirty vehicles in this convoy. That makes the chances of us getting hit about thirty to one. Those are pretty bad odds by any standards, wouldn't you say?"

"If we do take a hit, we have to leave the vehicle and set a perimeter. That greatly reduces the odds, doesn't it?"

"I'm of the opinion that Colonel Hussein is quite the 'been there done that' sort of chap. I doubt very much that he's going to be scratching his head wondering what to do. As a matter of fact, I would venture that he would welcome the opportunity to meet the enemy on a level playing field. There are quite a few of his men who may be just as enthusiastic."

"Even more of a reason for the insurgents to set a trap for him. If he's got a reputation for charging into battle, a smart opponent will take advantage."

"I almost hope we get into a scrape so the Colonel can prove his mettle. At the least, it'll send the rebels a message as to who they're up against."

"Don't you have a wife at home? Don't you have a very good reason for getting out of this in one piece?"

"I'll tell you, Lieutenant—"

"Jessica."

"Of course, Jessica. I think it might not be the worst thing for me to catch a piece of shrapnel in my arse. Tell me, did you volunteer for this mission?"

"On my level, it's usually something that's placed on your doorstep."

"Well, it was put in my lap by the Prime Minister. Something about me being on a short list. At first there's a tremendous feeling of pride, but when you receive these distinctions a couple of times you begin to wonder if they've run out of fellows who can perform a mission. Considering the fact that I'm in my thirties, I'm starting to think they've grown fond of calling the first number on the list."

"I can't say I don't feel flattered by getting the call. Yet I also consider the fact that if I'm on top of the list, the one behind me might not be as qualified to do the job."

"So you don't have anyone at home keeping a candle in the window?"

"Negative," she gazed out the passenger window. "It's the whole male thing in a nutshell. Eventually they feel as if they have to control the relationship. There comes a day when they try and tell you that you can't go out anymore. Maybe it's a challenge to their ego. They can't fathom why they're not the ones going out, and it's all downhill after that."

"Do you only date servicemen? Have you ever tried being with a civilian?"

"I tried early on. It just doesn't work. You're living in different worlds."

"Have you ever thought about becoming a civilian? You know, getting married, having children, the whole routine?"

"Not really. I'm not sure how I'd adapt to taking care of a baby, having dinner ready when my husband comes home. I can't really say I feel more comfortable sitting here with an AK-47 in my lap. There's got to be a balance somewhere, I've just got to find it."

"When you find it, you might be able to hold a seminar. I believe over half of the people in the service would benefit from the information."

"I imagine you've found it."

"Not quite. It's like that American gangster flick, *The Godfather*. I find my way out and they pull me back in."

"Lead vehicle pulling off the road," a distorted voice came through the CB radio on the dashboard. "Pull over and assume defensive positions."

The agents watched as Hussein's jeep began roaring towards a sand dune off to their left. William hit the brakes and they leaped from the vehicle, crouching alongside it and training their rifles on the jeep. At once they saw automatic fire coming from the dune just as Hussein and his driver jumped out and rolled across the sand. An RPG-7 fired a rocket into the jeep, causing it to erupt into a ball of flames. The convoy responded with a hail of 7.62mm rounds that routed the enemy from their ambush position. A cacophony of screams and secondary explosions encouraged the light vehicles to lurch from the road in pursuit.

"Take cover behind that armored truck," William motioned as he clambered back into the vehicle. "I'm going in to see what's back there."

"The suspense would kill me," Jessica vaulted into the seat alongside him.

"Did you not just say something about not wanting to leave the job for the one behind you?"

"You were saying something about the odds. It looks like Her Majesty's Secret Service will be going double or nothing here."

The truck bounded across the sand, its wheels spinning mightily to force its way through. They beheld a squad of guerrillas racing from their position, firing wildly at the approaching vehicles. One of them tossed a grenade which ripped one of the armored cars apart like a tin can. The other trucks focused their Russian-made PK machine guns on the fleeing terrorists and mowed them down behind the dune.

"It looks like they may have built a bunker inside the dune," William said as he circled around the side of the sand hill. "I want to go in and take a look. Maybe there's an identifiable feature that we can spot the next time."

"This might not be the best idea, William. There's always the chance they were set to prevent any flanking maneuvers from the road."

"That would be a grand idea if you were planning to defend your position. In this situation, they're about as ready to stay onside as a street team of three-card monte dealers."

Suddenly a mighty roar preceded a jolt that nearly turned their vehicle upside down. William's first instinct was to cradle Jessica's head, but a crushing blow to the side of his skull caused him to black out.

Khalid al-Nuzi and his platoon was camped outside Al-Qaim, an industrial town of a quarter million people. The town's primary function was to process phosphate from nearby Akashat until the facilities were bombed out by the Allies during the Invasion of Iraq. Afterwards, investors from India and Belgium arrived to build fertilizer and cement plants which reinvigorated the local economy. It was a prime target for the Islamic Army, which planned to acquisition its resources upon seizing control of the town.

"This is not the best situation," his lieutenant said as the leaders of the platoon sat around a campfire away from their subordinates. "There are fifty of us, and there are two hundred fifty people in that town. Certainly we can launch an attack, but if there is a sizeable militia force in the town we may be pursued into the desert."

"What choice do we have?" Khalid grimaced. "It is now or never. The Shiite government is teetering on the brink of collapse. Just as the Caliph says, this is the time for a final push. As we speak, the Americans and the Iranians are sending in thousands of their special forces units. The Russians are also sending aircraft and artillery pieces. If the Shiites are allowed to recover, once again we will be surrounded by their allies in Syria and Iran. This is our opportunity, my comrades."

"The Captain speaks the truth," the sergeant agreed. "How could we go back to our people and tell them that we did not act when the Islamic State depended on us? How can we go back to the discrimination and the injustice we have suffered at the hands of the Shiites and their American overlords? There is no choice but to strike in the name of Allah."

"My only concern is the reprisals our people face," the second lieutenant spoke. "The fanatics are crucifying Shiites along the countryside. Eventually they will seek revenge, as they did when they first came to power. It makes it all the more important that we win this war. Our families cannot endure another reign of terror."

"The worst part is that they are bringing those damned Kurds onto their side," said the first lieutenant. "The Shiites are cowards who run in the face of superior numbers. The Kurds fight to the death. How can those fools side with the dogs who treated them as badly as us after Saddam was overthrown?"

"The Kurds seek independence, just as we do," Khalid mused. "Over half of their lands overlap the Islamic State. The day of reckoning will arrive. They will become part of us or fall by the wayside."

"Why do the Kurds not join our cause?" the sergeant shook his head. "We are all Muslims, fighting for Allah. We have taken half of Syria and half of Iraq. With their help, we can destroy both Shiite regimes and focus our efforts in overrunning Iran itself."

"They believe they will emerge victorious in the long run. All the more reason for us to prove our superiority. We have the financing, the equipment and greater numbers. We must show them that resistance to our cause is futile."

"Captain," one of the men rushed over. "Someone has set a fire in the desert to the west of the camp."

"They should still be in plain sight," Khalid led his officers as they raced behind the soldier. "There is nothing beyond the desert but the Syrian border."

They beheld what appeared to be flaming lines in the sand about fifty yards ahead of them. They moved cautiously ahead as the platoon broke into squad formation and spread into a pincer movement. Most could not make sense of it, but a couple of

46

men could read English. They perceived the flaming letters in the sand to read: FIFH.

"What the hell does that mean?" Khalid growled. "That is not a word."

"Perhaps it is the Kurds demonstrating their illiteracy."

'Have a squad move out to each flank, and two squads up the middle with twenty yards between them," Khalid ordered. "Have them drop mortar shells around the flames. Allow them to burn so we can see what's out there."

The ISIL fighters had fought for over a year in Syria and were well-trained in the art of war. They quickly moved in a pincer on either side of the flaming sand that covered a fifteen-yard swath.

The two squads moving up the middle waited until the mortars hammered the area directly behind the flames. They worked a fire and movement pattern as one fire team laid down cover fire for the advancing group, leapfrogging one another until they were within yards of the flames ahead.

"Where are the cowardly dogs?" a corporal snarled, squinting as he peered through the flames. They could all see that pitch had been poured into the sand to ensure that it burned for an extended time.

"They ran like the curs they are!" one of the men yelled. "They—!"

At once a series of explosions reverberated through the night as claymore mines were detonated. They were set in the sand in front of the flames, facing eastward towards the ISIL campsite. Those closest to the flames were ripped to shreds as the ball bearings sliced through the air as shrapnel. A number of guerrillas dropped to the sand, cursing and screaming as the metal burned through their skin like a hot knife through butter.

"It's a trap!" Khalid yelled. "Hit the dirt!"

As the insurgents dove to the ground, four mortars popped from behind a nearby sand dune and scored direct hits upon their positions. Khalid realized this enemy was their equal on the field by the precision of this ambush. He would back out of the killing zone and let his sergeants give the orders, as snipers would be looking for the men in command. He reached the rear flanks where the platoon was situated and rolled into a depression from where he could view the field.

"Continue flanking the bastards!" Khalid yelled. "We need to encircle their position!"

"They're spread out behind the ridge just past the flames!" his lieutenant called back. "When our men come out of cover they're…"

Khalid stared in amazement as a sniper round ripped into the back of the lieutenant's head, causing his brains to spurt from his forehead across the sand.

"How many of them are there?" he screamed to the second lieutenant.

"It's impossible to tell. They are well covered behind that ridge, and I believe they are moving from place to place to confuse us. We have a number of wounded near the flames, and it's making it too easy to pick us off when we try to rescue them."

"Send men back to the trucks! We can overrun their position and hold the ridge while we pull our wounded to safety."

The soldiers closest to the truck got the signal and broke into a crouching run from their cover. Just as they reached the vehicles, a second round of mortars arched onto their position. There was a deafening series of secondary explosions as the trucks went up in a plume of flames, incinerating the insurgents as they tried to take cover. By now the ISIL fighters were trying to retreat but found themselves in a horseshoe bracket. Khalid tried to direct the retreat but was caught in the path of a concussion grenade that nearly knocked him unconscious.

Khalid spat blood as it began filling his throat. He tried crawling towards a nearby weapon but had a boot heel come down and crush his fingers. He cried out at looked up, unable to believe what he saw. A woman clad in black, her long black hair billowing in the wind, stood over him with an AK-47 propped on her hip.

"Is this all the Islamic Army has to defend themselves with?" she called out defiantly. "What kind of men are these who are so easily overrun?"

"The people in this war are *mujahedeen*," Khalid continued spitting blood onto the sand as it filled his throat. "We believe in Allah, in honor, in respect. You are a woman. You don't even belong here. Who are you? What do you believe in?"

She looked down at him as if inspecting an exotic insect.

"What do you believe in!" he screamed at her.

"I believe in anarchy," she smiled, placing the barrel of her rifle in his mouth. "I believe in chaos."

"Who are you?" he pulled away, blood running from his mouth.

"I am the Black Queen of the Citadel," she set her boot upon his chest. "And you are but an ant in the afterbirth of the New Revolution."

"It is not right that she humiliates a man in such a way," one of the Kurds said from a distance.

"She does have her moments," Jack Gawain smirked. "Best to let her play 'em up. You go prop the bastard up if ye like."

"Sunni dog!" the guerilla ran over as the Black Queen pranced away. "We only leave you alive so you can tell the tale of what happened to your pack of mongrels here!"

"It is best you finish me off here, you scum," Khalid managed as blood drooled down his chin. "If I see you again on the field of battle, by Allah's beard, I will cut your balls off and leave them in your mouth!"

"Tell the Sunni pigs in Al-Qaim that your dogs were scattered by FIFH."

"By *what*?"

"FIFH," the guerilla looked back uncertainly at Jack. "The Fearless Iranians From Hell."

"All right," Jack ordered. "Go ahead an' do 'im, then."

Khalid began praying to Allah as the Kurd walked around to stand over his head. To his astonishment, the guerilla pulled his pants down and took a shit on his face.

"Let it be known that this is how we feel about the mangy dogs of ISIL," the Black Queen called out over the writhing survivors of Khalid's platoon. "The next time we meet in battle, we will bury you in your own shit! Allah be praised! The messengers of Allah are FIFH!"

"FIFH!" the ambushers chanted as they left the field, firing their weapons into the air as they disappeared into the darkness. "FIFH!"

Khalid wiped the shit from his face as he wept and gnashed his teeth, praying to Allah that he would meet the Black Queen just one more time.

Mike Mc Cord and the Hammer of Allah pulled up to a small settlement outside of Al-Bab, which was a short distance from Aleppo. There was a violent reaction to the squad's attack on the camp at Mayer to the northeast of the city. The Syrian Army attributed the action to the Free Syrian Army and retaliated with a barrel bomb attack that nearly wiped out the camp the squad had terrorized. Mc Cord decided to enter the Al-Bab settlement en route to the Iraqi border.

Once again they arrived at sunrise, and they were met by a middle-aged man along the perimeter of the settlement. He seemed relatively fit, with gray hair and solid shoulders. Mc Cord and Qawi got out of the truck to meet him as he approached.

"Welcome, my friends," the man extended his hand. "My name is Paul. It appears everyone is still sleeping, but I am an early riser. Have you been driving all night?"

"Yes we have. We would like to fuel our truck and get some food for my men," Mc Cord replied after they shook hands and made introductions.

"Of course. Have them come out of the truck and I can find you a place to rest."

He watched as the ten mercenaries climbed out of the back of the truck. Qawi walked over and spoke to them quietly before they followed Paul and Mc Cord into the settlement. It was surrounded by a wall, though there were numerous points of access and no fences or gates. Most of the buildings were one story frame buildings with stucco veneers. The soldiers could see booths set up around the village square where a large fountain served as their water supply.

"Please wait here while I let my wife and daughter know we have visitors. They can prepare a meal and help make you comfortable."

"A wife and daughter," Qawi chuckled as Paul walked towards an adobe shack towards the far corner of the square. "Of course it'll depend on what they look like, but I'll probably end up with the daughter."

"You keep that thing in your pants until I say otherwise," Mc Cord admonished him. "The Free Syrian Army controls Al-Bab. They'll chase us across the border if they get the jump on us. I don't want to make any heavy contact until the men are fed and rested."

"So we'll do them up on the way out. Sounds like a plan to me."

Eventually Paul returned with a lovely dark-haired woman around his age and a pretty blonde teenage girl. They both carried a stack of plates, cups and utensils.

"This is my wife Sarah and my daughter Hannah. They will set tables for you over there at the picnic area. The food should be ready soon. Please have your men sit and relax."

"Is this a Sunni village?" Mc Cord asked as Qawi and the men followed the females to the tables beneath the patio cover along a walkway surrounding the square.

"No, we are Christians. We live independently of the towns-folk as best we can. Peaceful coexistence, it might be called."

Mc Cord watched as the commotion on the square caused people to emerge from their homes and begin preparing for the day ahead. His men were bemused as the vendors brought small baskets of fruit over to their table. Eventually the two tables where they sat were covered with snacks which they greatly enjoyed.

"So what side do you take in this conflict?" Mc Cord asked as he stood at a distance from the tables, where only Qawi re-frained from munching out on the delectable fruit.

"We take no sides. We live only to serve the Lord. As it is written, our kingdom is not of this world."

"There are Christian militias in Jdeidah at Aleppo. They fight to keep their women from being raped and their property stolen. You will eventually be forced to do the same."

"I apologize for differing with you, my friend. It is an all-powerful God who protects His people from harm. If He were to lift His hedge of protection from around us, then it would not be ours to question. The ways of God are beyond human comprehension."

"You don't believe Allah is God, do you?" Mc Cord hooked his thumbs in his gunbelt.

"It is written that the only way to salvation is through the Lord Jesus Christ."

"So why aren't you trying to witness to these Muslims?"

"Men do not convert others, it is the Holy Ghost who brings men to Christ. We will not break laws or argue with men to change their beliefs. If we did, we would be removed from here. There would be no place for men to come to learn about Christ if they chose to do so."

"I come from a Christian town in Texas. I went to an evangelical church. They taught that we were to go out and bring men to Christ."

"Every man has his own ministry and his own purpose within the Body of Christ. Some are led to evangelize, others to teach, and there are those who simply pray. Only God can question what is in a man's heart."

"That's pretty well your Get Out Of Jail Card, isn't it? 'It is written', huh?"

"The Holy Bible is what the Lord uses to speak to men. It is our only guide. It is our means of communication with the Holy Ghost."

"You certainly know your stuff," Mc Cord grinned as Qawi came over.

"So are we gonna take this place down?" Qawi asked as Mc Cord stepped aside with him.

They spoke in English so Paul did not understand.

"I'm talking to this man. Looks like the women are bringing the food. I want the men to eat their fill and bring some fruit back with them."

"What the hell? I told you I wanted a piece of those women."

"And I told you to keep that thing in your pants," Mc Cord stared into his eyes. "Are you questioning my orders?"

"Negative, sir."

"Then you have them fill their canteens and take a basket of fruit each. After they're finished eating you take them back to the truck."

"Yes, sir."

Mc Cord watched Qawi return to his table before turning back to Paul.

"Will you not eat with your men?"

"When you are on the field, you do not want to make room in your stomach for food you don't have when you are hungry again. They will learn the hard way."

"What made you lose your faith, brother?"

"What?" Mc Cord asked incredulously, then looked away. "Life. War. The world. You just start drifting away from it. It's a gradual process. Just like you. You drifted towards it gradually, did you not?"

"I did, my friend. You may have drifted away, but you never drift so far that God cannot reach you."

"I do not know about that. Besides, what happens when He does not want to reach you?"

"He loves one child just as He loves all His children. He will never turn His back on you. He will wait until you finally turn your face to His. No matter how long He has to wait, when you finally turn to Him, He will be there."

"You really think He will wait that long?"

"Pray with me. Say hello to Him before you leave."

Qawi watched in amazement as Mc Cord and Paul stood by the fountain with their heads bowed. He turned and joined the others as they collected their gear and the fruit baskets. They returned to the truck and waited until Mc Cord rejoined them.

"Hey," Qawi said as Mc Cord gunned the engine. "I apologize for what happened back there. I don't know what got into me."

"No problem. It was the Devil made you do it."

"What's that?"

"Nothing worth talking about."

Mc Cord hit the gas pedal, leaving the Christian settlement outside Al-Bab in the dust behind them.

Chapter Four

Debbie Cantor woke up to find herself hogtied, her wrists and ankles bound together behind her back. She remembered being injected with morphine to render her unconscious. It was now that she felt the unbearable heat and the burning of her wrists from the tightly knotted ropes. She sensed that she was in a metal container, and began rolling around to reach a wall and get her bearings. If she could find a durable sharp object it would be enough to give her a fighting chance.

She adjusted her vision to the blackness, beams of light streaming in from apertures in the container. She made it to a side wall and rolled so that her shoulders were against it. The metal was hot and burned her bare arms. Her legs were soggy from the sweat-drenched fatigues that encased her lower torso, though she could feel her socks and knew they had only removed her boots. If she could keep from banging around there was a chance she could make something happen.

At once the door to the container was thrown open, and two riflemen rushed into the metal structure. They grabbed Debbie by the arms and dragged her out, tossing her so that she rolled down a metal ramp to the sand.

"So the Jew bitch has awakened," a man scoffed. "Let us hear what she has to say for herself."

"I am not a Jew and I am not a bitch," she called out in a hoarse voice. "I'm on an intelligence gathering mission with the United Nations. We heard rumors of activity near the uranium mine at Akashat. Regardless of whether you're with the Iraqi Army or ISIS, the development of uranium-based weapons are a major violation of international law."

"She speaks Arabic well," a man walked around and stopped where his boot was within inches of her face. "Our fingerprint check comes back with nothing, which usually indicates an intelligence operative. She may be a Jew, although it is just as likely she could be an American or an Englishwoman, possibly EUROPOL. We could beat it out of her, but she will have an established alibi in place. Perhaps if we threw acid in her face and put a photo on the Internet, someone would come forth and arrange for a ransom."

"That would be the stupidest thing you could do!" she cried out. "Something like that would tell them I gave up everything. There would be no reason for them to want me back after that."

"Let us quit jerking around," Mahomet Qawi walked up and kicked sand into Debbie's face. "You have been given orders from Ayatollah Qom Diabolus to hand the whore over to us. You can stall by waiting for word from the Caliph Al-Baghdadi, but you do not want to make enemies of us. Surrender the whore so that we can take responsibility for what happens after this."

"Quit calling me a whore!" Debbie spat sand out of her mouth. "This is an outrage! My name is Debbie Magee, and I am a British citizen assigned to the United Nations as a political advisor! I have diplomatic immunity!"

"There you have it," Qawi smiled. "When you let the rutting slut run her mouth long enough, you learn everything you need to know. We will hold her for ransom against the British imperialists. If they do not pay the full sum, we will negotiate piece by piece. We will start with her fingers."

"I eat bacon!" she yelled. "You will sin against Allah!"

"Silence, whore!" Qawi kicked her softly in the head. "Pick this tramp up and load her into our truck. We will take her back to our hideout and negotiate terms with the Jews in the British Parliament. Perhaps I will allow the bitch to jerk me off along the way."

"I do not have the means to satisfy you," she said as two militants yanked her off the ground.

"And what is that, you cunt?"

"I would need tweezers and a magnifying glass."

Qawi responded with a crushing right that plunged Debbie into unconsciousness.

William Shanahan woke up to an electric shock down his spinal cord which paralyzed him with indescribable pain. He tried to roll to his side and the shock returned, causing him to drop back in helpless resignation.

"Did you have an injury before you took this assignment?" he heard the voice of Jessica Anderson at his bedside. "I'm not one for raghead prognostics, but I daresay they are confirming a previous assessment that you are well aware of."

"I'm not coming out," William hissed. "They were well aware of my condition when they sent me in. I'll finish this job, and when we're done you'll be a reliable source as to why I shouldn't go out again."

"Are you mad?" she insisted. "You've got fractures along your vertebrae. Your missus had to be stupid if she did not notice it. I'm going to call in and request that you be returned to the UK immediately."

"I do a lot of hydrocodone. I kept a bottle in the medicine cabinet and one in the car. She suspected that it was one reason why they gave me a desk job."

"You apparently did a hell of an acting job."

"Also, I'd appreciate it if you never bring her up again."

"No problem."

"Plus I'm staying in. You used to run with the big dogs, you weren't one of them. You need someone with my experience out there. The Peshmerga are great when they have a good coach behind them. If they get caught in a jam with some rookie who can't call plays, they'll cut and run. Don't do anything stupid. I want to stay out here with you. Take advantage of it."

"I heard you were still here in the trailer," Colonel Hussein knocked before he came in. "I hope you are still in working order."

After the rocket attack, Hussein's men annihilated the ISIL guerillas before withdrawing to Tal Afar. They were ill-received by the locals who were sympathetic to the Sunni rebellion. They kept moving until they came across a Kurdish settlement, where they were given provisions along with access to their facilities. William was brought there and attended to by a physical therapist, the closest thing they had to a doctor.

"I always compare it to being in a tough football game," William replied airily. "You tape the fellow up, give him some painkillers and get him back on the field. It's not over until it's over, as the Yanks say."

"The therapist said you were suffering from severe back pain and may have suffered some kind of spinal injury. I can have you taken to Baghdad for treatment."

"You mean Baghdad's still up and running?"

"As best we know."

"I appreciate your concern, Colonel, but the Lieutenant and I have an important assignment here. I can't afford to leave her here on her own. If you were to make contact with Mustafa Hilal while I was away, she might be forced to take unacceptable risks. The sooner we can get this chore taken care of, the sooner I can get back to England and seek treatment."

"You know, we have received word overnight of a team similar to yours working in this area. Only they are working with the Iranians, which brings credence to your superiors' theory. If the Shiites and the Sunnis are both recruiting from abroad, it is exacerbating our problem. It is quite possible that it is not only the Caliphate issuing a worldwide call for the *jihad.*"

"Mercenaries?"

"There was a woman described to be similar in features and physical attributes to the Lieutenant. She was also backed by an Englishman. Their unit ambushed an ISIL unit and told the survivors they had been overrun by FIFH, the Fearless Iranians From Hell. The woman identified herself as the Black Queen. She had a pronounced European accent."

"Bloody hell," William hissed. "It's Jack and Lucretia. O'Shaughnessy would've told me if they were here. They must've gone over the fence. Yet I know Jack too well. He would've never done such a thing."

"You have worked with these people before?" Hussein asked.

"I can't go into detail, they were classified operations," William replied. "One thing about Jack: he would have 'God and Country' written on his tombstone. Whatever he is doing can't be going against the Crown's interests. I suggest we spread the word of his presence throughout the Peshmerga network. If anyone comes across him, he should be detained or monitored until we can catch up with him."

"Do you consider him a threat?"

"They're both extremely dangerous. I would inform your men to avoid direct contact and to notify us immediately should he be located."

"Very well, I'll spread the word," Hussein exited the trailer.

"We have to contact the Office and see what O'Shaughnessy has on this," Jessica insisted.

"That's a negative. If Jack's working with the Shiites and MI6 is unaware of it, they may start probing and put his life in danger."

"Don't you think we have some sort of obligation here?"

"Yes we do, and that's why we're being discreet. He may have some information that may be of use to us. As a matter of fact, I'm quite sure he does."

"I get the feeling that this is the least place on earth you'd want to be in, but for some strange reason, wild horses couldn't drag you away."

"I don't like leaving loose ends behind. Especially where lives are concerned."

"You're the last boy scout, aren't you?" she teased.

"That's what Jack used to say," he managed a grin.

The Fearless Iranians had taken refuge near Lake Assad near the Tabqa Dam west of Al-Thawrah. Jack Gawain went out of his way to find a place near the lake as Lucretia was entirely distracted by the heat. She had trained with ex-Foreign Legionnaires in Algiers with the Citadel years ago. Only she had not traveled with twelve men in an M-113 armored personnel carrier in the Syrian Desert at one hundred ten degree temperatures. She had taken one rib too many by the well-meaning Kurds, and nearly pulled a knife on one of them before Jack decided to stop.

"Well, yer lookin' none th' less for wear, lass," Jack smiled as she returned from a stream running from the lake. "Th' picture of loveliness."

"Is that supposed to be a fucking joke?" she demanded. Her long black hair was tied back in a sopping-wet tail that hung down her back like a mop. She wore only a tanktop and her camouflage tactical pants, causing the men to avert their gaze as she stormed past them. Her eyes were as blue sapphire, gleaming at him like exploding stars.

"Now don't get yer panties twisted on my behalf," he replied. "I'm th' one who found this place o' rest. I'm sure those fellows had no problem smellin' somethin' fishy."

"You bastard!" she screeched, diving at his throat. He grabbed her wrists as he fell backwards, holding her patiently until she ran out of gas.

"Are ye done, love? Y'know, yer quite beautiful when yer upset."

"*Mon dieu*," she exhaled, rolling off Jack and using his rippled midsection as a pillow. "I can't believe we were in SoHo just a couple of weeks ago. There must be a way out of this."

"Well, if we cut an' run, we can still live off our savin's, but there's not too many nations where the CIA or MI6 can't go lookin' fer us. That dirty bomb in th' Eiffel Tower wasn't yer best moment, darlin'. They'll be after ye forever an' a day unless we pay the tab."

"You don't have to be part of it," she turned her head to gaze into his eyes. "You can cut me loose and go in on your own."

"Aye, but I'm hooked on ye, girl," he stroked her cheek. "That face, that body."

"I'll grow old one day."

"Ye'll still be the Black Queen. My Black Queen."

"Do you love me, Jack?" she rolled over and propped her chin on her hands as they laid across his midsection.

"Nay, I'm just testin' me skills for lack of anythin' better t'do," he sighed lazily. "Besides, killin' this raghead bastard would be a solid contribution t'God an' country. Y'know, makin' right fer all my days of lawlessness, as they put it."

"So it's not about me."

"Nay, why would I be roastin' me arse out here on account of you, woman?"

"You're a liar."

"Yer a bitch, an' a right hot one at that."

She rolled and was straddling his chest in one move, having pulled her combat knife and placed it against his jugular vein. The men began rushing over but he waved them off.

"Just her way of showin' affection, lads," he called over before he grabbed her wrists and rolled her over. He pressed his lips against her mouth as they laughingly walked away.

"Yea, an' I'll repay evil with love," he peered into her eyes before rolling away from her. "T'was Saint Patrick or some other Fenian bastard who said it, as I recall."

"I'll never understand your people or your religion, just as I'll never understand you," she breathed deeply of the scent of grass and the breeze from the lake. She pulled her knees up and enjoyed the feel of the grass against her bare feet.

"Aye, well, we don't understand ourselves much either," he smiled. "Well, we'd better get t'discussin' plans with th' fellas before it gets dark. I don't want t'be sittin' near any of these shanty towns when th' sun goes down."

The couple rejoined the squad under the shade of a patio cover where a card table had been set out along with a map.

"We are but within a few miles of Manbij," Sergeant Munif pointed to a spot on the map. "It is not far from where we received reports of an ISIL sighting at Al-Bab. They went into a Christian settlement but did not attack. According to witnesses, they fit the description of the squad that committed the atrocities at Mayer. If this is a gang of foreign mercenaries, then it would stand to reason they will be reporting to Mustafa Hilal."

"Why don't we just capture them and force them to reveal Hilal's location?" Lucretia asked.

"Put it this way, love," Jack arched his eyebrows. 'You remember the jackpot we ran into at the Carcassonne when that Russian Spetsnaz squad went headlong into yer French Foreign Legion team at the Citadel. There were bodies lyin' everywhere when it was o'er. It's hard to place sure bets when All-Star teams are involved. Not t'mention we're not fer certain how good these fellas are."

"I think you would be pleasantly surprised," one of the Kurds spoke up. "Bear in mind that we went up against Saddam Hussein's Republican Guards during Operation Desert Storm, plus we've come out on top against the Free Syrian Army, Al Qaeda and both the ISIL and ISIS. We are not a force to be trifled with, my friend."

"Well, maybe we can toss a little salt on their tails an' see what happens," Jack mused. "We can figure out their reaction time, capabilities, defensive patterns, all th' good stuff. Aw reet, then, let's come up with a plan, then figure out where the bastards may turn up next."

The men that FIFH were discussing were meeting at a Hima cooperative due north of the city of Ar-Raqqah. The Bedouin settlement featured a sizeable area covered by tents which the nomads used for lodging and administration. They avoided political issues as much as possible and did not want to offend the Sunnis by denying their request. As a result, Mustafa Hilal was escorted by an armed squad to the cooperative where the Hammer of Allah team awaited.

"There are two very important issues we must discuss, praise Allah," Mustafa revealed as he, Mc Cord and Qawi met in a spacious carnival tent. "The first thing to address is a statement released from the Pope at the Vatican today. He has announced that he wishes to meet with the Caliph in order to discuss world peace. He has suggested that he may be open to establishing a concordat with the Islamic State."

"Glory be to Allah and his messenger, the Caliph!" Qawi was exultant. "This will lead to the world recognizing the Caliphate and creating a true spiritual mecca for all Muslims."

"Yes, this is a very important step, but we must not be too optimistic. Remember that the Great Satan has already appointed its gang of murderers at the Pentagon to make plans to assassinate the Caliph by use of its drone aircraft. Although this Pope is politically adroit, he will not want to make enemies with the

Americans. We will have to see how the Americans react to this message before making plans."

"Well, since you're bringing it up, what did you have in mind?" Mc Cord asked.

"The Ayatollah suggests that we volunteer our services to act as the Caliph's personal bodyguard should the meeting be scheduled. It would be a show of force, allowing the world media to see the quality of soldiers at our disposal."

"Sounds kinda stupid to me. Not only do we lose our classified status, but our pictures will probably go viral on the Internet. You know there are more than a few of the boys who are wanted for war crimes. Not to mention the guys who are wanted for military and criminal charges."

"I think you both know that the Shiites have a price on my head for having led my platoon into abandoning the Iraqi Army for the cause of Islam," Qawi grimaced.

"Perhaps you could wear balaclavas for dramatic effect," Mustafa mused. "We can allow the press limited access so they can see that you represent different nations of the world."

"Better have the place surrounded by rocket launchers," Mc Cord grunted. "I'll be damned if I'm gonna stand up there alongside the Caliph with an armed drone zeroing in on my ass."

"Rest assured we will take all the necessary precautions when the time comes. Another thing to consider is that having the Pope would guarantee a strike-free zone. Can you imagine the American President claiming responsibility for having smoked the Pope?"

"It would be the first time he took responsibility for anything in a coon's age."

"Coon's age?"

"Now don't tell me you called me all the way out to the middle of nowhere to ask me to babysit the Pope and the Caliph at a time to be announced."

"Actually there is a more pressing matter at hand. Our forces outside Muthanna have captured another chemical weapons stockpile."

"Aw, bullshit! You guys took one near there months ago and there wasn't enough active chemicals there to kill a damn fly."

"Not this time, my friend. This is an underground depot that Saddam Hussein was planning to use in case of emergency, only the Americans were in Baghdad before the Shiites had a chance to deploy the weapons. We have obtained about a dozen sarin gas bombs."

"Well, that sounds good. So what are you gonna do, steal a plane so we can drop them on Baghdad?"

"We are planning to combine them into three large bombs that we will detonate within the capitol cities of the Great Satan: Washington DC, New York and London."

"And what, you're not even gonna ask for money first?"

"True believers do not trade in filthy lucre. We strike in the name of Allah in exchange for his blessings and a place in his Paradise."

"So what part will we play in that grand scheme?"

"Should everything go as planned, we will split your squad into three fire teams, each responsible for delivery of the devices."

"That would be worth a hell of a lot more money."

"We would think so. We would pay a hundred thousand per man."

"For that I'd put it in the Statue of Liberty's crown."

"We were thinking Wall Street," Mustafa grinned evilly.

"Look, we've got priorities here. I've got one of my people being held by ISIL. Most likely she's been taken for ransom, or to obtain more information which she obviously doesn't have. This whole thing starts and ends with that damned uranium mine, and we've got to hunt them down to get her back."

"I agree we've got priorities, Mr. Frantz," Lieutenant Farid Gorgan was condescending. "I realize your people are highly concerned about your colleague, and you will not reconcile yourself to the fact I told you so. You and the woman went out to the mine without clearance despite the fact this is a joint operation. You were separated and she was captured. Your first assumption is that the terrorists have confirmed the existence of accessible uranium in the mine. Well, we know there is uranium in the mine. That's why they call it a uranium mine."

"Don't screw around with me, Lieutenant."

"You can call me Farid."

"Okay, Farid. There's a big difference between uranium fifty feet beneath the ground and ore that's already been brought up by trams into storage rooms. You know the Hussein regime would have been extremely cautious in bringing up heavy tonnage. They would've been avoiding US satellite surveillance. If he would've had it brought it up in huge quantities, the Americans would've suspected he was trying to build a nuclear bomb. Now you got the Shiite regime in power, but they don't need the uranium because they're already building a bomb in Iraq."

"That's one thing about Britons," Farid grinned, looking at the sand and shaking his head. "You are so well-informed on world affairs that the lowest field soldier can engage in a heated debate on any number of earth-shaking events. Unfortunately for us Iranians, it is not ours to offer our opinions or lend advice to our superiors. In this case, our mission is to ensure that the terrorists are unable to retrieve WMDs from caches hidden by the Hussein regime. Just because they abducted your partner does not confirm the presence of usable material."

"Why would they take her? Why not just blow her head off? They know the Crown won't negotiate with terrorists. They won't pay a pound for her return. They're using her for bait. They're trying to lead us somewhere. Are you telling me you don't think it's worth trying to find out where and for what?"

"This is personal for you, Mr. Frantz."

"You can call me Glenn."

"Your relationship with the woman," Farid's eyes glinted evilly. "She is very beautiful, is she not? You Europeans hold yourselves so far above us, as if our desires and dreams are so far beneath you. Yet it is such a basic need, a common cause. You want to rescue the woman because you cannot stand the thought of her being ravished by the bandits. Admit it, my friend."

"You're trying to turn this into something it's not."

"It's about the pussy, Glenn, the pussy. I want to hear you say it!"

"Okay," he lowered his head. "It's about the pussy."

"Excellent!" Farid clapped him on the shoulder. "As long as I have a tangible reason to put my men in harm's way in rescuing your sweetheart from the terrorists. I will send word to my superiors that MI6 suspects there is uranium ore beneath the surface waiting to be shipped. Just as long as we are both aware of the real stakes on the table."

"Whatever you say."

"Come," Farid said as he headed back towards where the men were lounging around their armored personnel carriers. "Let me inform the men as to their new objective."

Glenn followed Farid over to where the squads were mustering. He had a terrible taste in his mouth, feeling as if somehow he had done Debbie a grave injustice.

Debbie Cantor remained bound after spending her third night in the captivity of the ISIL fighters. Upon her release by the Hammer of Allah, she was taken into the mines by an ISIL squad ordered to keep her hostage until further notice. So far it had not been such a tribulation as the mine was cooler than the surface temperature. They had been left with an abundance of water containers. It was the prevailing attitude of her captors that bothered her. They knew that the Iraqis would not attempt to destroy the mine as they desperately wanted to recapture it. They prayed to Allah that the Americans would not subject it to a drone strike as a matter of their national interests.

"You," one on the men came over to where she was tethered. "Are you hungry?"

"No," she moaned. "I'm lonely and I'm scared."

"It will all be over soon," the guerilla assured her, coming closer to see her pretty face. "Our leaders will pray to Allah for the right decision in this matter."

"I've been all alone here with no one to talk to, not a friendly face, not even a smile or a hug. You don't know how terrible it makes me feel."

"You must endure, woman. It is for the best."

"Do you have a woman? Do you know what it's like for her when you're gone?"

"Yes," he lied, having been brought up in a strict Muslim community that worsened when the radicals moved in. "I am not entirely unsympathetic."

"Won't you just give me a hug?" she asked plaintively, facing him on her knees. "I just need to have some physical contact with someone. I can please a man, if you know what I mean."

His blood began simmering as he considered her offer. It was well-known that infidel women loved to perform fellatio. He would have preferred to have sex with her right there, but if his comrades came across them he would be ruined. Yet if she was only giving him oral sex, he could push her away and cover himself before anyone could see what was happening.

"All right, woman," he came forth and exposed himself. "I have what you want."

Within three minutes, the mujahideen warrior had come to the end of his life. Debbie unbuckled his pants and loosed his combat knife simultaneously, driving the blade between his legs as soon as he dropped his pants. The guerilla dropped to the dirt and died of shock as Debbie ran deeper into the mine, looking for an avenue of escape.

Chapter Five

It was daybreak when the sentries along the perimeter of the camp Colonel Hussein's platoon sounded the alarm. They were situated around ten miles west of Tal Afar and found themselves under attack by a platoon of ISIL soldiers. The enemy used the cover of darkness to surround the camp, having them pinned in on four sides. Hussein's squads set up defensive positions using their armored personnel carriers as cover. What they did not know was that ISIL had summoned a tank from a nearby encampment to assist in routing the Kurds.

William and Jessica had been encouraged to remain in the rear with the gear as Hussein's squads broke out to confront the attackers. The riflemen holding down the northeast position were forcing the guerillas to take cover behind nearby sand dunes within a hundred yards of the campsite. Only there was a lull in the action, and when William grabbed a pair of binoculars he could not believe what he was seeing. An M1 Abrams tank was emerging from behind one of the dunes, grinding its way through the sand while providing cover for the insurgents.

"That turret's swinging around!" William signaled Jessica to cover as he ran towards a nearby armored troop carrier. "Everyone get back, get away from the truck! Now!"

The Kurds watched as the big 120mm cannon drew a bead on their APC, then dove for cover as the tank lobbed a shell directly into the carrier. There was a deafening road as the round tore into the vehicle, causing a secondary explosion as a white-hot shard hit the fuel tank. Two of the Kurds screamed as burning metal ripped through their flesh. The others rolled for cover as they began returning fire against the guerrillas crouching behind the tank.

"Spread out, try and flank them to the left!" William yelled at a Kurd corporal. "We'll try to pick them off from the right!"

William then broke into a crouching run to where Jessica was crouched near a short row of sandbags. He dove as the insurgents caught sight of him, a lightning bolt of pain shooting up his spine as he hit the sand alongside her.

"All right, then, you're done," Jessica jacked a clip into her M-16, taken aback by the look of pain on William's face. "Just sit tight here, I'll see if I can distract them on their right flank."

"No," he insisted "Help me get up on my knees. If I don't twist my body I'll be fine."

"Why not put your pistol in your mouth and spare us both the trouble?"

He hissed with pain as he rolled to his knees, then focused himself on the tank rolling steadily towards the flaming truck. Its machine gun was pinning the Kurds down, causing them to split into three fire teams. One team attempted to flank the oncoming tank to the left while the second team laid down cover fire. The third team moved towards Jessica and William, creating a diversion that allowed the agents to sprint to the right flank.

"I think we can get to the tank if the Kurds try a full press," William winced.

"You're asking them to commit suicide."

"They're not stupid. If we make the first move they'll pull the bandits offside."

With that, William jumped to his feet and signaled a charge, running in a crouch to his right. The ISIL fighters turned their rifles on him, losing their cover behind the moving tank in the process. As William expected, the Kurds rushed the left side of the oncoming tank, raking the guerillas with automatic fire. The tank gunner and his right flank guards were caught in a fierce exchange with the Kurds on their side, unable to support the riflemen being cut down on the left flank. It allowed the Kurds to rush the tank, compromising the machine gunner who had to turn his weapon around to deal with the charging enemy.

It was the break William and Jessica were waiting for. Jessica rolled across the sand, vaulting to her feet and sending a burst of rifle fire at the tank gunner. It ripped across his left side, causing him to fall from the tank and drop lifeless on the sand. William and the Kurds charged the unprotected left side of the tank, giving William enough time to toss a grenade down its cannon. The Kurds dove for cover as the turret erupted in flames, killing the four-man crew inside.

"Well," Jessica opened the front of her shirt, allowing a faint breeze to cool her generous breasts. "I think I'll put you in for a Victoria Cross."

"Don't bother," William dropped to one knee as the Kurds rushed up the middle of the battlefield, overwhelming the insurgents who were retreating from their center position. "I've already got one."

"Impressive," Hussein came over to them.

"I certainly thought so," Jessica agreed.

"I meant the view," Hussein nodded at her bosom. "I'd prefer that you button up. I'll get you some extra water."

"No, that's fine," Jessica buttoned her blouse. "Did you flank them?"

"My men are mopping up as we speak. There's a Kurdish village northwest of here. I think we had better bring our wounded in and resupply. Hopefully there's another APC somewhere we can requisition."

"Your men are everything we've heard they were," William smiled. "Even with a tank advantage the terrs were no match for them."

"We fight for Kurdistan," Hussein was proud. "It is our wish that when you come back this time next year, all the land north of the 38th Parallel will be part of our independent nation."

"It is my wish that you'll have me and my wife flown in to your capitol city for a second honeymoon."

"Let us hope we are still around for it," Hussein grinned, clapping him on the back. Jessica watched as William winced before they exchanged smiles.

Calling this mission a pain in the back was becoming an understatement.

Khalid Al-Nuzi was riding shotgun with Mike Mc Cord as their armored personnel carrier lumbered its way westward from Al-Qaim. Qawi and the Filipino, Ernesto Guzman, led the way in a Desert Patrol Vehicle mounted with an M60 machine gun. Al-Nuzi had been debriefed by ranking ISIL officers in Al-Qaim after being ambushed by FIFH. Shortly afterwards they contacted Mustafa Hilal, who in turn called Mc Cord.

"There is a renegade team of Shiites in the vicinity of Al-Qaim that ambushed one of our patrols last night," Mustafa informed him. "They left a survivor to give us a message. If we do not respond promptly, they will take it as a sign of weakness. There are Europeans on the team, a male and female. Obviously they are part of an MI6 mission."

"They don't have a whole lot of options. They keep running west and they'll be going straight into the Syrian war. They start moving north and they'll be in Turkey. They move south and they'll run right into our people or the Kurds, either way. They double back and they come to me."

"This time we want pictures. I want you to stack their heads up and take pictures we can put on the Internet. We will post them on our website to discourage these crusaders. You will make an example of them for the British people. When they see this, they will rise in protest against their leaders for getting them into a third Iraqi conflict."

"Yeah, well, don't you worry about it. I'll carve this bunch up nice and pretty, like a Christmas turkey. And I can assure you, the boys on this team'll be fighting amongst themselves to be the one who does the honors."

"I place all my trust in you, Mc Cord. I know Allah smiles upon you."

"Don't worry about a thing, buddy. We're gonna make Allah real happy."

As they drove along, they saw a deserted settlement to the south. There were heavy planks seated upon cinder blocks which were left behind by the previous inhabitants. The only building that remained intact was a stucco veneer mosque at the far end of the clearing. Behind that was a rocky hill shrouded by desert foliage.

"Think there might be a well in there somewhere?"

"Perhaps," Khalid replied. "We are but minutes from the border. It may be a good idea to allow your men to rest. You will want them to be fresh when we catch up with those Shiite dogs."

"Hell, we'll get to stretch our legs when we catch up with those ragheads," Mc Cord grunted. "Fearless Iranians From Hell? We're gonna take 'em down like a bunch of animals escaped from the zoo."

"I caution you not to take them lightly. They are highly disciplined and very well coordinated. They took out an entire platoon of my men."

"I don't wanna hurt your feelings, but it's like Barack Hussein once said. This is gonna be like the college varsity going up against the NBA All-Stars. The only thing that'll be left of them is a pile of heads and that curry stink."

"Varsity? NBA?"

"Hey, lemme ask you something. It is true they shit on your head?"

Just before Khalid let loose, the heard the sound of hail thumping against the side of the vehicle.

"Mc Cord?" Qawi's voice came in on the CB radio. "We're taking fire from that abandoned settlement on our left."

"Get Guzman on that M60 and return fire!" Mc Cord barked before throwing open the rear window of the cab. "Huttig, get up on that M60 and spray that damn lot! I'm going straight on in there. Rest of you guys, get ready to deploy!"

"You got it," the big German replied, throwing open the side door of the APC. He scrambled up to the deck, and signaled Guzman so that they simultaneously poured automatic fire at the abandoned settlement about a hundred yards away. Mc Cord and Qawi swung their vehicles around and had them bouncing across the sand toward the target site

"You take the lead," Mc Cord ordered Qawi. "Hans, you get the big gun ready if we take fire from the mosque!"

"Roger that," replied Huttig, wearing a headset. He replaced the M60 on the tripod with a Mark 19 40mm grenade launcher, ready to fire on command. Qawi cursed and swore as he gunned the engine, knowing they would take the brunt of an explosion if a trap had been set by the ambushers.

There was a brick wall on either side of the entranceway, which had been corroded by the desert over the decades. As the DPV rumbled through the entrance, a tripwire activated grenades on either side of the wall. Only Qawi and Huttig found themselves drenched in putrid waste as portable toilets had been set by the gateway. The toilets were torn asunder by the explosives, showering them with the horrid mixture.

"They hit us with the waste from the toilets!" Qawi choked and gagged as he veered off to the left. "I'll cover you, bring the truck in!"

At once they took rifle fire from the mosque, and Mc Cord parked the APC in the entrance so that his men could take cover on either side of the brick walls. Huttig lobbed a 40mm shell at the mosque, blowing the doors and most of the front walls off the building. Mc Cord could hear the distant roar behind the building and realized what had happened.

"Check out the mosque," he ordered the team, who circled the building from both sides. "I'm pretty sure they cleared out. You're gonna find motorcycle tracks at the rear of the building."

Qawi and Huttig rushed over to the well at the center of the settlement, then fell back cursing as a cloud of flies belched forth from the depths. As it turned out, the Iraqi Army had tossed a dead pig into the well to discourage Sunnis from returning to the area. The fighters stripped down to their briefs, stomping their uniforms into the dirt so it could absorb some of the slime. They next sacrificed some of their canteen water to wash their heads and hands. They exchanged insults with their comrades as they climbed back into the DPV.

"It is as you said," the Frenchman, Yves St. Laurent, came over after having checked out the mosque. "The snipers were on motorcycles. We see their tracks criss-crossing across the dunes so we couldn't tell how many there were. I suspect there were at least a dozen of them."

"Well, I'm sure we haven't heard the last of them. We'll follow the tracks and see where it takes up. At least we know one thing for sure."

"What's that?"

"I always thought Qawi was full of shit. At least I can say for fact that's he's covered in it."

The air was filled with blasphemous oaths as the ISIL squad searched the abandoned mine with flashlights, searching for the elusive Debbie Cantor. They found the knife driven through his crotch and could see the look of agony on his face when he died.

There were two chambers carved into the rock along either side of the main shaft that descended at a thirty-degree angle to the next level. Two of the fighters progressed cautiously down the shaft, walking alongside the railway for about twenty yards before retreating.

"There is no way the bitch would have gone much further," one of the men spat grime from his mouth. "The air is thick with dust and it is dark as the grave. I say we toss a grenade down there and bury her alive. If we go down there it will just encourage her to climb away from us."

"You know they'll never approve it," a comrade shook his head. "The Caliph has ordered that production resumes here as soon as we liberate it from the Shiites. If we drop a grenade it'll set them back for weeks. We will merely set up watch at the mine entrance and wait her out. She will either die of hunger of thirst, or give herself up."

"Hey, assholes," they heard a voice near the cavern entrance. They turned in alarm and saw the silhouette of a woman in the darkness.

"Look!" they cried. "It is the bitch!"

"I'm glad you mentioned al-Baghdadi's plans," she called, striking a match and touching it to the short end of the fuse on a bundle of dynamite. "Looks like I'll be killing two birds with one stone…or stick."

They raised their weapons and began firing as Debbie vaulted for cover. At once there was a deafening roar as the five sticks of dynamite she found in the shaft exploded. It caused the beams supporting the shaft to split asunder, resulting in the entire chamber to collapse in an avalanche of rock. Debbie waited for a short time before heading to the squad's APC, gunning the engine and heading off south towards Baghdad.

Lieutenant Farid Gorgan arrived at the abandoned mine a couple of hours later after receiving a message from a nearby Iraqi reconnaissance unit. They reported the blast and suggested that Gorgan's platoon check it out to see whether ISIL forces would be moving in to assess the damage.

"Certainly if the dogs were planning to lay claim to the mine after they captured the territory, they would come out to estimate how much work it would take to reopen it," Gorgan told Glenn Frantz as they bounced along the dirt road leading to the mine in a four-passenger DPV. "By Muhammad's bones, if that mine ends up in anyone's territory, it will be Shiite."

"This is going to turn into a bloodbath out here," Glenn stared at the shimmering heat waves along the sunbaked horizon. "You know the Iraqi government's not gonna cut their losses out here. Neither are the Kurds if they finally declare independence. Plus, consider the fact that al-Baghdadi's already declared this area as part of the Islamic State. If all three forces show up out here, not to mention the Revolutionary Guard, this could be what Saddam once called the 'mother of all battles'."

"Hah!" Gorgan spat into the wind to his right as the jeep raised a cloud of sand in its wake. "We will chase the insurgents like swine into the desert. The Syrians will flee right behind them if they choose to live. Once we reclaim the northern land, the Kurds will also walk away with their tails between their legs. It is just as you have seen, no one dares stand up against the Shiites. We have respected authority and taken counsel with the Americans long enough. Now that the US has left the field, it is time for us to take what is ours."

Almost as if on cue, a hail of bullets rained down upon the lead APC at the head of the convoy. The vehicle ground to a halt as the driver called Gorgan on his CB radio.

"What are you seeing out there?" Gorgan demanded.

"Just muzzle flashes," the driver replied. "It almost seems as if they were warning shots."

"Get our signal officer up front. Give the dogs my cell phone number."

Glenn hopped out of the jeep and watched bemusedly as the signal officer trotted to the fore. He began flashing Morse code to the enemy force lying ahead in the desert night. After a short while, there was a response. He looked back and saw the soldiers standing around their APCs, sipping water from their canteens as they awaited further developments. It was not long before Gorgan got a call on his cell phone, and he walked away from the convoy as his captains stood by.

Glenn stared bleakly at the mountain range that was a vast shadow in the darkness. He only prayed that the terrorists had not decided to keep her hostage inside the mine. He and Debbie had gone through boot camp together as well as commando training. They had known each other since grade school, and had it not been for Sarah, well, who could know. She was his best friend and his lifelong partner, and he would not rest until he learned of her fate.

"Ho!"

Gorgan called out to his captains and lieutenants. "The high ground has been taken by the Kurds! It appears Colonel Hussein himself was in the area, and rushed to be the first to report what happened. Send in one of the APCs, and let them know I'll be right behind them."

One of the lieutenants signaled the lead vehicle, and his squad piled back into the truck to meet with the Kurds. They only prayed it was not a well-planned ISIL trap. If the unit surrounding the mine were actually Sunni, they would be riding to their deaths. Most of them closed their eyes and prayed to Allah as the APC lurched towards the uranium mine.

At length they could see a number of lights flashing from the vehicles parked around the mountainside. The engine of a DPV suddenly began growling as it cruised steadily towards where the lead APC was parked. The occupants exchanged words with Gorgan's men before clambering out. The four men smiled and waved as they came face to face with Gorgan and his captains.

"Lieutenant Gorgan. I have heard a lot about you. I am Colonel Hussein. This is Captain Shanahan and Lieutenant Anderson of the CIA. We are escorting them on a reconnaissance mission."

They all exchanged handshakes as Glenn approached.

"We too are providing an armed guard for our special guests. This is Lieutenant Frantz of MI6," Gorgan made the introduction.

"Lieutenant Frantz," William stepped forth. "May I have a word?"

Gorgan ordered his men to set camp for the night, building a bonfire as the Kurds drove in from the mountainside. Jessica watched from a distance as William and Glenn walked beyond earshot.

"So you're the real MI6ers," Glenn smiled.

"And you're our friends from Tel Aviv. Where's your partner?"

"I pray she's not beneath the rubble over there. She was the kidnap victim."

"We hadn't heard anything about it. Should we send for an excavation crew?"

"That might be a good idea. I'm not counting Debbie out yet. That girl's got plenty of tricks up her sleeve."

The agents returned to the campsite, hoping that she had at least one left.

Chapter Six

Debbie Cantor began moving due east after blowing up the mine entrance at Akashat. She figured she might be able to reach the Euphrates and negotiate a ride downriver towards Baghdad. If she could get hold of a phone she could contact the Mossad and get reconnected with Glenn. Regardless of how it worked out, she had to get out of the desert. A woman getting caught out here alone wearing military fatigues had the chance of a snowball in hell.

The ISIL fighter was carrying a CZ-99 Yugoslavian automatic pistol, which she traded for the knife she shoved up his crotch. The magazine carried fifteen rounds, which would be enough to get her out of most jams. She grievously regretted not having looked for water but if she had been intercepted, it might have cost her life. She knew that dying of thirst in the desert was far more preferable than being raped and butchered.

She remembered when she was going through basic training and discussed the option of suicide when faced with an impossible situation. She mentioned to the instructor that she learned in Beis Yaakov[1] that the rabbis theorized the suicides at Masada were forgiven by God as the only way out of an impossible sit-

---

1. female religious school

uation. The instructor surprised her by giving her a tap on the cheek in rebuke.

"What would have happened if the Jews in the Holocaust had all decided it was the only way out of an impossible situation? I would not be here, you would probably not be here. All this —the state of Israel— would not be here. I would not presume to argue with a rabbi, but it is my uneducated opinion that one loses all faith in God by ending their own life. Can you think of a situation where you would lose all your faith in God, Deborah?"

The desert, as anyone who lived in the Middle East knew, was one of the damnedest places to live on Earth. It routinely hit over a hundred degrees every day, but with nothing to block the night wind, it could cool down to the low sixties in hours. If the wind was strong enough to carry sand, it could whip a dust storm that could bury someone alive. Right now it was making her wish she had at least looked for a jacket before she left the damned mine. It made her shiver when she stopped, but when she kept moving her standard Iraqi combat boots were killing her feet.

Plus, moving through the sand was torture. She dared not follow the road as if she got spotted by enemy, it would have been impossible to escape.

Factoring in all the things that could have gone wrong would have paralyzed her on the spot. She would have found a rock to crawl under until the crack of dawn. After that, she would have lost track of everything and became a wanderer in the desert, stumbling along until she collapsed or was captured. You had to think like every nomad who had ever crossed this land. If thousands upon thousands before her had done it, then somehow she would join the ranks.

Glenn had long ago stopped teasing her about being the son her father never had. She had stopped beating herself up over phallus envy long before that. Regardless of all the psychological implications, she never apologized for being a tomboy for life. She never wished she was a man or lost any desire for them.

She was just very comfortable being a woman in a man's world and enjoyed the challenge of competing against them and winning. One day she might find a man who could accept that, and who knows. Until then, she was never going to look back at her life and regret the path she had chosen. And she was damned sure not going to start now.

She had just decided to take off her boots to see if going barefoot would have made it easier when she heard the sound of a truck engine. She cursed herself for not spotting it on the road but realized the driver was using infrared goggles to go undetected. That meant they were probably Islamic Army in having no fear of being picked up by the Iraqi Army in this region. She started to hit the dirt when they shone a spotlight directly on her location.

"Lieutenant Cantrell," a Southern accent blared through a loudspeaker. "Saw your work back at the mine. All is forgiven, but you need to come out now. If we gotta come out and get you, it's gonna get rough. I don't care about them ragheads, but I'm responsible for my boys. If anyone gets hurt picking you up, I can't hold 'em back."

She realized this was the same team that she was turned over to when she was first captured. These were probably the mercenaries it was rumored ISIL was hiring. They had bigger fish to fry and most likely were picking her up as a routine matter. Still, this was a bullet in the head moment. She had killed one of theirs and escaped, and she knew there was something going on at the supposedly abandoned mine. She was now a liability, and she had to decide whether she would want to go on their terms or hers.

"Show your weapon and drop it, put your hands behind your head," the voice ordered as the truck rumbled towards her with its headlights on. "We won't ask again."

Debbie fought every instinct in holding out the pistol and dropping it, doing as she was told. Two men jumped from the back of the truck and bound her hands behind her back with industrial plastic ties. They next forced a thick bit into her mouth and placed a nylon sack over her head before dragging her back to the truck.

The stench of body odor was nauseating as the men shoved her to the floor between them. All she could do was offer up prayers to Yahweh as the truck gunned its engine and rumbled away.

William Shanahan took a walk with Glenn Frantz that brought them beyond the earshot of both the Kurdish and Iranian platoons camped precariously alongside one another. The rival groups had met each other on the battlefield at the turn of the century and there was no love lost between them. Colonel Hussein was discussing the situation with Captain Shiraz of Quds Force, trying to figure out a way for them to work together in hunting down the Islamic Army's mercenary unit. It seemed evident that they were policing the abandoned uranium mine and would probably be entrusted to move the insurgents' WMDs once they were ready for use.

"It appears we're finally finding some common ground," William nodded towards the command tent where Hussein and Shiraz were meeting. "My superiors specified that our mission was to take out Mustafa Hilal and disrupt the foreign mercenary network. They implied that you and your partner would be meeting up with us to expedite the mission. They hadn't specified the WMDs, but if the mercenaries' trail leads to uranium or sarin bombs, well, by all means."

"The door swings both ways, especially with all the high-level double-talk," Glenn replied. "They are highly concerned over chemical or nuclear weapons that could be used against Israel. If those mercenaries are standing in our way, it goes without saying they will have to be obliterated. It's like they give you a work order and transportation and let you figure out the rest."

"I know the feeling. Speaking of which, what kind of feedback are you getting from the Iranians? I understand you and your partner are posing as MI6 agents. God forbid those Iranians should find out they're providing security for Israeli agents."

"It's working so far. The problem I have is that my partner's an MIA. She went on a recon detail inside an abandoned uranium mine and disappeared. We have reports that the mine entrance got blown up the other night. I'm betting my bottom dollar that she escaped and got recaptured."

"That's the mine at Akashat. Our people were concerned that ISIL had reactivated the mine. They may have brought the mercs in to provide security for the project. We know ISIL's taken more than a couple of Saddam's chemical factories, but most of them were dismantled by UN security forces. They may be able to salvage some of the facilities in time. Getting their hands on uranium would give them an immediate advantage."

"Our sentiments exactly. Debbie had one of her hunches and insisted on checking out the mine after we camped for the night. She promised she was going to just poke around and left me behind so as not to alert the Iranians. That was the last I saw of her. I held off reporting it to Shiraz, and the next thing I knew there was a report there was an explosion at the mine."

"I'm just wondering how you didn't report it immediately after your partner – a female at that – went missing."

"You don't know Debbie Cantor," Glenn stared into his eyes.

"What kind of work did you do together before they sent you here?"

"She's undercover. She develops our situation, draws the target into a favorable position. I'm her sniper."

"What's it like?"

"We're the best. Sometimes we get it done in a matter of hours. Once it took over a week. High-level Hezbollah chieftain in Lebanon who had twenty-four hour security. She jumped through hoops to get him in the open by himself. We finally got him."

"You ever miss?"

"Never. How do you do with your partner?"

"I don't know. We haven't had any action outside of driving over a homemade mine. I got the worst of that."

They caught sight of a Kurdish warrior trotting towards them. They were informed that Colonel Hussein was waiting to see them.

"We've come to a peaceable agreement," Hussein informed them as they took a seat at the folding chairs in front of Hussein's luncheon table in the spacious tent. "The Shiites will guard our flanks as we proceed west to the Syrian border. It only makes sense as we outnumber them two to one. We will travel past the mine at Akashat to determine whether the insurgents are attempting to reopen the mine. Once we reach the border we will request Iraqi air support if it is in our interests to cross into Syria."

"In your interests?" William squinted. "Your leaders have a deal with my government. If we don't neutralize Mustafa Hilal and disrupt his network, the oil barons will pay millions to have mercenaries brought in from all over the planet. He's probably got enough men already to infiltrate and paralyze Baghdad. The longer you wait, the stronger he gets. If you wait long enough, they'll get so big it'll take an army to stop him."

"Only you forget, my friend. Those Iranians have an ace in the hole that they are not declaring. I know how to play poker, you see. I learned from the Americans."

"Just wonderful. And what might that ace in the hole be?"

"FIFH," Hussein grinned broadly. "It is our understanding that they all already in Syria. Surely the Iranians are merely awaiting the signal. Once FIFH disrupts the mercenaries' logistical system, we can pinpoint their location and call in an airstrike.

All you will have to do is take Hilal's picture on your cell phone. If you can identify his body, that is."

"He's got it all figured out," Glenn frowned as they left Hussein's tent. "What the hell is FIFH, anyway?"

"I'm hoping beyond hope it's an old friend who's finally got his act together," William shook his head. They walked over to where the Kurds and Shiites were resolving their differences in a game of soccer.

At least it was a start.

Debbie Cantor had spent one of the worst nights of her life.

Once the truck began rolling, her blouse was pulled up and her bra pulled down. After that, her large melons had been subjected to every possible abuse. They were squeezed, sucked, pinched, punched, bit and burned. The abuse went on for hours until the truck finally pulled over near an abandoned campsite just outside the Syrian border.

"If you mention anything to Mc Cord," she was warned as they pulled her clothing back over her torso, "we'll cut them off next time."

They kept her bound and gagged as they led her to the campsite. Four of the men quickly set up a command tent where they began preparing a campfire and arranging their cooking utensils. They drove a stake into the ground and fastened her to it away from the sun so she did not suffer more than necessary.

"The bastards have caused the mine to collapse," the Russian called Arkoff grunted. "The Islamic Army will have to bring up a bulldozer and a construction crew to repair the damage. This is going to set us back a week."

"The Ayatollah won't wanna hear that," Mc Cord growled. "He says now's the perfect time to strike. With all that shit going down on the Russian border with the Ukraine and Israel at war with Hamas, the Americans aren't gonna commit to another war here in Iraq. If we can hit them with a dirty bomb, we can get them to withdraw long enough for us to win this war."

"We're going to have those sarin bombs any time now," Van Damme the South African was confident. "We've already recovered two of Saddam's old storage bases. We're bound to come across one with launch-ready weapons. The ones we have will be functional once we can get them to Lebanon or Yemen for an overhaul."

"The old man wants to be able to strike next week," Mc Cord insisted. "If we don't come up with something soon, he's gonna come down on Hilal, and Hilal's gonna come down on me. I know if we don't come up with something soon, he's gonna get another team out here. That's gonna cause that bonus money to spread thin. Now, I'm a greedy man. I don't like to share, especially when there's no need. Now, if that mine could be blown down, I say we can blow it back open. We need to get them ragheads down there to get us some uranium."

"I've got some experience with diamond mines back home," Van Damme pointed out. "Something like that can go either way. You may be able to blow the entrance back open. On the other hand, another explosion could cause further damage to the mine shaft and result in another cave-in. We could end up getting set back for a month instead of weeks."

"That sounds a whole lot like a coin toss," Mc Cord decided. "Well, I'm a gambling man. I guess we're gonna have to take that chance. You get on the horn with Hilal and tell him I need a truckload of explosives out here."

"You're going to need a team to accompany it. Unless you're going to do the honors," Arkoff pointed out.

"Hell, the Englishman Turnbull is a demo man. Rest of you can lend a hand. We'll open that hole and make it wide like a riverboat whore. Once it's open we'll set up there in the hills and keep an eye on it until ISIL and their mining crew show up."

"I just hope our luck holds out. The Iraqi Army's been on the counteroffensive all week. They've got Tikrit surrounded and they're bombing the hell out of Mosul. If they take back both those cities, their next move will be to push ISIL back into Syria. And we'll be going right along with them."

"That's why we need to get that uranium, boys. If our guys can set off a dirty bomb anywhere on the East Coast in the US, the American public'll force them to cut and run. Just like what happened in Lebanon in the Nineties. Once those Special Forces boys pack it in, those Iraqi Army boys're gonna run back to Baghdad with their tails between their legs."

"What about her?" Arkoff jerked a thumb towards where Debbie laid.

"If Hilal doesn't want her, you boys can have her. You don't think I know what was going on in back of that truck last night? Hell, it was all I could do to keep Qawi from jumping out and getting in on it."

"She better hope England changes its mind about dealing with terrorists," Van Damme chuckled as he walked off.

"Hey, Mike," Flores the Salvadoran called from the truck. "I got Hilal on the radio."

"Mustafa," Mc Cord grabbed the hand mic.

"Have you retaken the mine?"

"I don't see where we ever lost it. We've been policing the central border out here all week, we pretty well got everything nailed down. The local communities are shitting bricks when we drive by, and we haven't seen hide nor hair of the Iraqi Army. We heard reports of your boys having taken a couple of Saddam's chemical arsenals back."

"What about that mine, Mike?" Mustafa insisted.

"Look, there hasn't been any activity at the mine, nobody's been working it, so we weren't focused on it. We caught a lone MI6 agent out there and turned her over to an ISIL unit. She escaped and sabotaged the mine entrance in the process, but we got her back. I'm gonna bring her in so you can cut a deal with the English for her."

"Her? You mean to say it's a woman?"

"Yep. I reckon you're gonna be tearing somebody a new asshole over that."

"Are you sure she has no further means of escape?"

"Hell, I got her bound and gagged with a bag over her head, tied to a stake in the middle of the camp. Superman couldn't get her out of this mess."

"Very good, Mike. I knew I could count on you. You're my right hand man out there. The Ayatollah is depending on you."

"Tell you what, right now the mine is inaccessible. I'm gonna need a truck of dynamite out here to get it back open."

"What? What happened?"

"This bitch tossed a stick in the shaft on the way out. Buried your boys alive. I'm figuring I can blow it back open and keep watch until your miners show up."

"We can't afford any further damage to the mine, Mike."

"Don't worry about it. I'll have that thing spread wide as a whore on Friday night."

"What?"

"I'll get 'er open, Mustafa, don't sweat it. You just have your techs in Lebanon or Yemen or wherever ready to go to work. We'll have that mine up and running, you can count on that."

"Good. I'll have the dynamite brought out tonight. Once you get it reopened, our miners will be there the next morning."

Things were moving a lot quicker than McCord had expected. He knew the Ayatollah was preaching on the need for a dirty bomb attack on America, but didn't think it was coming this soon. It wasn't that he gave a damn. He lost that feeling after going AWOL in Afghanistan upon learning he was going to be indicted for war crimes a couple of years ago. He only hoped that it would go the way the Islamic State thought it would.

Otherwise he and his team would be on the run for the rest of their lives.

Glenn Frantz sat in the DPV alongside Jessica Anderson, filled with reservations as William Shanahan came over to see them off. The agents had discussed this option at length, and Glenn felt as if he had been bulldozed into this deal. Only sitting here between the bickering Kurds and Shiites accomplished nothing. The uranium mine seemed to be the entrance to the abyss, the gates of Hell to whoever dared breach them. Maybe that was why no one wanted to lay claim to it. Most likely the first one to claim it would be trampled by all those rushing in behind them.

"This should be a piece of cake for you both," William tried to reassure them. "If you two go out and claim to be UN inspectors, even ISIL won't be reckless enough to try and snatch you."

"This is a lame-ass, half-baked plan, in my opinion," Glenn frowned as he gunned the engine of the jeep. "If we run into an ISIL unit we're going to end up wherever Debbie is. Somebody needs to slap those two prima donnas around and make them get with the program."

"Any suggestions?" William was blunt. "Look, this country is on the brink of civil war. There's no one *to* call. The Kurds aren't a nation, they're an amalgamation of tribes. I'll bet Hussein doesn't even know who he's taking orders from. As far as the Iranians, they're probably working here on the same terms we are. The main line to the Quds Force Command goes straight to voice mail."

"So the entire war's gonna revolve around everyone waiting to see who's gonna claim that mine?" Glenn demanded.

"ISIL's got half their troops tied up in Syria trying to wedge themselves in between the Syrian Army and the Free Syria rebels. Their ISIS force is trying to hold Tikrit and Mosul. That mine is in the middle of a power vacuum. No one's strong enough to go inand take it. The only way anyone'll make a move is if someone else decides to be king of the hill."

"Come on, we're sitting here wasting petrol," Jessica insisted. "Let's get on with it."

The DPV began rumbling down the road, and there was about ten minutes of silence before Jessica broke the ice.

"You two are pretty close, aren't you?"

"We've been working together a long time."

"It seems a bit deeper than that."

"How so?"

"It seems as if you're in the grieving process. It tells me that you've lost someone very dear to you, and you've already given her up for dead."

"Well, we've known each other since we were kids. We volunteered at the same time, and we signed up with Sayeret Matkel[2] together. We both received offers from the Mossad around the same time. They just thought it made sense to pair us up. I don't think she's dead. I think she blew up the mine to escape the other night. I'm just wondering what she's going through right now if she hasn't made it back yet."

"Lots of things could have happened. She might have hooked up with Bedouins. She might've had to go undercover in a settlement. She might be doing recon on another target."

"Lot of mights there."

"Well, then, put on your happy face, fellow. Don't write her off just yet."

"East for you to say. Look, how do you want to play this? If I take the high ground I might be spotted by a recon drone. If I drop you off it's gonna look pretty obvious."

"That case of yours can pass for camera equipment. If you drop me off and set up a short distance away, someone might believe you're surveying the landscape. I'd suggest you assemble

---

2. Israeli Special Forces

your rifle, then tuck it out of sight and stand fiddling with your cell phone while keeping an eye on me with your binoculars. I'm quite sure that's as innocuous as we're going to get."

"I like that accent. Are you from London?"

"Born and raised. You sound like a Yank."

"Both my parents came over from America. So did Debbie's. You know what they say, birds of a feather. American Jews and European Jews tend to stick with their own kind. They just have more in common culturally. The kids are the ones who bring them together. Debbie and I hung out with lots of European Jews and Russian Jews. After a while the parents got acquainted at school activities and community events. It's probably like that everywhere."

"Not so much. There's been a large influx of Muslims in England since Y2K, and both communities have put up their defenses. Your parents never say anything, but you can tell by their attitude there's a problem. Not mine, specifically, but friends and relatives. When you've got one Muslim friend too many, they have an attitude like, don't you have friends of your own kind to hang out with? It's a real sticky wicket. I can sit here and talk about it all day."

"Hold on," Glenn said, slowing the jeep. "What's that?"

They stared apprehensively to their left as a huge dust cloud began swirling along the horizon. They spotted a DPV, then saw another and another behind it. Following the jeeps was a line of APCs, and the agents realized a convoy of at least platoon strength was roaring straight in their direction.

"Holy shit," Glenn hissed. "You tell them I picked you up outside Al-Qaim and I was driving you to Akashat."

"And what good do you think that'll do?"

"Play the UN observer angle. I'll think of something to cover my ass."

"You're not one for thinking on your feet, are you?"

They watched in astonishment as the convoy roared past them, sending clouds of sand billowing into the sky. It seemed almost as if they were responding to a fire alarm in the middle of the desert.

"You think they're ignoring us?" Jessica quipped.

"I've never been so insulted," Glenn switched off the engine as the agents sat back and watched the dust storm roll by.

An hour earlier, an Islamic Army convoy was triumphantly bringing a truckload of sarin gas cylinders from central Iraq into Syria. They had driven off an Iraqi battalion from a settlement outside Tikrit and recovered two bunkers filled with chemical weapons munitions, as well as a former production facility. The Iraqis knew the location of the facility and the bunkers, though keeping it top secret to avoid a confrontation with their allies. As a result, the government would not report the capture of the WMDs by ISIL.

The lead vehicle, flying the black flag of the Islamic Army, bounced along the sand with a 40mm machine gun on deck. It was followed by four DPVs and four APCs which transported a platoon of hardened guerillas. They had notified Mustafa Hilal of their acquisition, who in turn informed the Ayatollah Qom Diabolus. The evil cleric ordered that the weapons be brought to his stronghold outside Mayer for an all-out assault on Aleppo. He intended that one would be kept behind.

Its destination would be New York City.

"The Ayatollah will be glorified in the eyes of Allah for his accomplishments!" the captain crowed as they bounced along the sandy road. "Not only will we deliver a crippling blow to the Syrian Army in Aleppo, but we will strike a blow against the Great Satan in New York City. There are nothing but yellow dogs trying to protect these chemical weapons depots from us. We will continue to drive the scum across the desert until the Caliphate extends from Syria to Iraq."

"I know it is not for us to discuss," the lieutenant said nervously, "but there is talk that the Ayatollah may ascend to the position of Caliph if his great works overshadow those of Al-Baghdadi."

"Of course it is not for us to discuss!" the captain was adamant. "Whoever holds the title of Caliph sits at the right hand of Allah along with his messenger, Muhammad! Whether the Ayatollah can exceed the Caliph, this I do not know. What I know is this: the Gospel of Barnabas predicts the return of Muhammad as prophesied by the prophet Jesus Christ. Once Muhammad returns, he alone will draw the Caliph to his side as Allah rules and reigns forever and ever!"

They saw the rocklines on either side of the road but had never considered the possibility of an ambush in such an isolated area against so formidable a convoy. It was the heavy impact of a bump in the road that made them realize they had drawn their last breath.

There was a deafening explosion as those in the convoy watched in astonishment while the lead vehicle disintegrated before their eyes. The bodies of the passengers were tossed through the air as chunks of burning meat. The DPVs behind the lead vehicle slammed on their brakes as did the trucks behind them. The drivers began barking furiously into their CB radios but were interrupted by the echoes of explosions behind them.

The ambushers were firing RPG-7 rocket launchers into the trucks at the rear, ripping the vehicles asunder. The two APCs had been reduced to flaming wrecks, effectively sealing off the pathway so that the other trucks could not escape. The passengers began jumping out of the cars and were raked with automatic fire from the top of the rock walls. The Islamic Army fighters tried to defend themselves to no avail. Within minutes it was over, and forty-six guerillas lay dead in the shallow passageway.

"FIFH!" the ambushers chanted victoriously. "FIFH!"

Jack Gawain and Lucretia Carcosa climbed down from the rock walls, directing traffic as their Kurd warriors got in the front and rear vehicles bracketed by the flaming wrecks. They gunned the engines and rammed the burning trucks out of the way so that the trapped vehicles could be steered clear of the killing zone.

"Jack!" Lucretia waved as she peered into one of the salvaged trucks. "I found it! The gas canisters are here!"

One of the greatest challenges facing the Islamic Army was that they were accepting all comers into their ranks. Recruits were interrogated as to their Islamic beliefs and dedication to the cause before an Internet background check was made. After that, they were armed and assigned to a guerrilla unit. It allowed for the insertion of double agents by their enemies, and both the CIA and MI6 had more than a few of their spies placed among the ranks of the mujahideen. As a result, the CIA were advised as to the acquisition of the chemical weapons, which they passed on to Jack.

"Simply fantastic," Jack marveled at the tanks. They appeared as acetylene tanks, over two dozen packed upright in the bed of the truck. They were padded by mattresses wrapped in tarpaulin and tied down by thick ropes. "We are going to have quite a time setting these things off."

"Where are you planning to use them?" one of the Kurds asked.

"Well, they want us to do the Ayatollah in, and we'll have to find out where he's hiding to do that," Jack mused. "I think we'll have to get him so pissed that he'll get on the Internet and ask all his friends to finish us off. That way the CIA can get a fix on him and get us an address. I suppose we'd better go out and pick a spot that'll really yank his beard."

The Kurds gave joyous thanks and praise to Allah as they climbed into their truck.

Jack and Lucretia turned the vehicle loaded with sarin gas around, set on returning it to the people who sent it out on its mission of mass destruction.

Chapter Seven

Not far from Aleppo, a squad of Islamic Army fighters had escorted Mustafa Hilal to the mountain lair of Ayatollah Qom Diabolus. They had been summoned to attend a hearing of a case involving a family who had been accused of harboring infidels. Complicating matters was the fact that it involved one of Hilal's most trusted soldiers. Mohmad Aladdin had been one of those who trained the mercenaries of the Hammer of Allah, which made the offense all the more serious.

They arrived at the entrance to the cavern where they left their weapons with a security squad. A cleric led them into the winding tunnel which brought them to the throne room. The air was thick with the odor of burning pitch, bated with the scent of frankincense. They followed the imam into the great chamber, whose walls were made of lava which ascended to the heavens. The floor appeared as a great pool of black marble which glistened like glass. Torches flickered along the walls, dimly illuminating the shadowy room. In the distance was a great dais upon which sat a golden throne. Upon it sat the fearsome Qom Diabolus.

"Hear ye and come forth, all who have come to witness the justice and mercy of Allah!" a cleric came forth to stand at the edge of the dais. "The great and terrible Ayatollah will grant forgiveness for the remission of sins to whoever proves themselves worthy."

The dais was surrounded by another squad of fighters, along with a group of civilians to the left and an obese man in robes to the right. Everyone including Hilal and his men dropped to their knees and pounded their foreheads against the marbled floor in praise of Allah.

"All rise!" the imam ordered them. "We bring before Allah the case of the Aladdin family. They are accused of giving food and shelter to Christians under siege of the Army of Allah!"

"Great Ayatollah, have mercy!" the woman cried out as her husband, both sons and her daughter trembled behind her. "We have known these people all our lives. They are good neighbors who helped us countless times when we were in need. The Islamic Army burned their homes and they had no place to go. We merely gave them food and let them stay with us until they could make arrangements to move to another city."

"Do you not know that when Allah condemns the infidel, no man or woman can save them!" the Ayatollah bellowed from his lofty throne. "How dare you attempt to meddle in the affairs of the almighty?"

"I am the one to blame, let me be held accountable," her oldest son stepped forth in front of her. "I am a member of the mujahideen. I convinced my comrades to let the Christians be when my family gave them refuge. If I had not intervened, they would have taken the Christians and none of this would have ever happened."

"So," the Ayatollah snarled. "It is you who are guilty of this crime."

"Yes, O Great One."

With that, the Ayatollah stretched his arm towards the young man, his fingers pointing at the accused. His eyes rolled up in their sockets, and his mouth uttered arcane curses unheard of for many centuries. At once there was a loud snapping noise, as if the sound of a tree limb breaking. Mohmad Aladdin stiffened, then fell dead to the floor with a broken neck.

"My son!" the mother cried out, falling to the floor alongside her son as her husband and her son knelt alongside her. "If only you had taken me instead of him!"

"So! If that is your wish, so be it!" the Ayatollah narrowed his eyes. Once again he gestured and suddenly the mother, father and brother of Aladdin exploded into flames. The lone survivor screamed in terror, watching as her family was burned alive by the demonic fire.

"Let this girl be taken into an Islamic home where she can be raised in the ways of Allah!" the Ayatollah commanded. "Mahmet, she will be placed in your custody to the end of her days!"

"Oh, thank you, Great One!" the blubbery man at the far end of the dais clapped his hands. He was a cleric from Al-Bab where he had a palatial estate inherited from his family. It was well-known that he had a harem of eighty-eight wives kept prisoner in a row of barracks on his land. Each of them had been awarded to him by Islamic courts. "I will enlighten her in the ways of Allah!"

"Oh, please, Great One, take my life now!" the beautiful girl wailed. "I would rather you kill me than give me to that man!"

"Silence, you insolent wench!" the Ayatollah roared. "Or I will have your nose cut off to forever remind you of your impudence!"

"No, no, that won't be necessary," the fat man insisted, instructing two of the soldiers to take the girl away. She screamed and cried as the warriors grabbed her arms and dragged her from the chamber.

"Are there any more who seek the justice of Allah?" he called out.

"No, your Greatness, we are not worthy!" the cleric responded.

"Go in peace," the Ayatollah commanded.

At that, the congregation dropped to their knees and dropped their foreheads to the floor in praise of Allah.

"Who is this man that who performs such great works in the name of Allah?" they asked as each of them returned to their own homes.

And so the argument continued as to whether the Ayatollah should replace Al-Baghdadi as the Great Caliph of the Muslims.

"According to reports, there is a great concentration of Islamic Army fighters near Akashat," Colonel Hussein pointed to a map on his desk in his command tent. "One of their convoys were ambushed along the road, and it has caused them great concern. As we speak, they are massing troops along the border so that the ambushers cannot escape. It is said that they are bringing elite troops in as backup in case the Iraqi Army tries to exploit the situation."

"Damn it," William Shanahan shook his head. "If we had air or artillery support we could take them out with a coordinated strike. They're ripe for the taking."

"The convoy we saw was at least platoon strength," Glenn Frantz confirmed. "They were armed to the teeth. They had heavy machine guns, recoilless rifles and rocket launchers. If ISIL is bringing up those kind of reinforcements, they'll wipe out anything the Iraqis could throw at them."

"Plus, consider the fact that they're on the other side of the border," Jessica Anderson pointed out. "The Iraqis couldn't pull off an air strike if they wanted to without invading Syrian air space. If we notified the Syrians, they might take the opportunity to wipe out some of the Sunni settlements near the border. That could result in even more Sunnis taking up arms and joining ISIL."

"I don't see any other option than to take them on ourselves," Hussein massaged his bearded chin. "I can spread the word among the tribal leaders throughout Kurdistan. They will sweep in from the north and force the rebels to come up and meet them. It will shift their balance of power so that we can hit them in what would become their right flank. If we can trust these Shiites to protect our left flank, perhaps they can sweep in a circular pattern and hit them from the rear. The guerrillas will have no choice but to retreat towards the Syrian border. Either they will be reinforced by the Free Syrian Army, or perhaps the Syrian government's border patrol will join on our behalf. It is what you Westerners call a crap shoot."

"I think it's our best opportunity," William reasoned. "If we're successful, all three of us can achieve our goals. If the terrorists catch up with the ambushers and retake the chemical weapons, it'll give Glenn a chance to destroy the sarin bombs before they can smuggle them across the border. If the mercenary force takes a hand in the battle, I'll have a chance to take a prisoner and find out where Mustafa Hilal is holed up. As for you, Colonel, a battle of this magnitude should ensure that the Islamic Army will be crippled for some time to come."

"Very well," Hussein exhaled tautly. "Glenn, have the Shiite leader come in so we can put a plan together. I will have my men contact the local tribes and prepare them for this battle."

"Excellent," William nodded. "The three of us will start making our plans as well."

"Nice going, Captain," Jessica was sarcastic. "Maybe the three of us can protect the flanks of the Quds Force."

"Well, actually, that's what I had in mind," William replied as they walked towards the western perimeter of the camp.

"What?"

"Consider this," he explained to them. "The Islamic Army has superior equipment and they've had combat experience, but I doubt they're well versed in military science. If and when the Kurds sweep down from the north, chances are they'll throw everything they have at them. Their commanders have a healthy fear of the Kurds. They know the Kurds are fearless warriors who never retreat. They won't be worried about covering their flanks, which is the break Hussein will need. If they get hit hard on two sides, they'll certainly call for reinforcements. They may reinforce with battalion strength, and if they do, it'll be for all the marbles."

"Both you and Hussein have some high hopes," Glenn was doubtful. "If the Kurds don't show up in force, we may end up getting routed. It'll give ISIL all the time they need to move those chemical weapons south. If they bring them into Lebanon and put them in the hands of Hezbollah, it could turn into a disaster for Israel. The stakes are too high, William."

"What do you suggest, Glenn? Isn't that why we're here? My government isn't going to make another commitment to this conflict. Even if they were moving a nuclear weapon, England doesn't have the military authority to block it. Even the Americans haven't committed to any military options. We're all alone here, old man. We're the Dutch boys with their fingers in the dike. We've got to make this work."

"Okay, so how are we going to cover Quds Force?" Jessica interjected.

"We sweep along their left flank, circle northward and take up a position along the high ground," William knelt down and drew a diagram in the sand. "Glenn's a crack sniper, he can cover us while we go down with RPG-7s and determine which trucks may be carrying the sarin tanks. That is, if they've intercepted the ambushers by then."

"I have little doubt that they will," Glenn noted. "If you saw them hauling ass the way Jessica and I did, it's probably just a question of how far from the border they ran them down."

Mike Mc Cord and the Hammer of Allah had been radioed by Mustafa Hilal shortly after the judgment of Allah had been rendered against the Aladdin family. He had been advised of the ambush of the sarin gas transport and was ordered to recover it by all means necessary. Mustafa dispatched the Hammer of Allah unit to deploy along the border as an elite company of Islamic Army guerillas swept westward from south central Iraq. Mc Cord's men would be reinforced by a battalion coming in from the west from the outskirts of Aleppo. They would bracket the ambushers and have enough might to bring the WMDs back to Lebanon regardless of what the Syrian Army might do to stop them.

"All right, lady, time's running out," Mc Cord growled as the APC bounded across the sandy road headed northeast. Debbie Cantor's wrists and ankles were shackled as she sat beside him. She had not bathed for days and felt wretched alongside him, but would not show any weakness before her captors. "For the last time, I need to know where your unit was located and what their battle strength is. If you don't start talking, Qawi's gonna strip you naked and tie you spread-eagled on top of the hood of this truck. Talk about a human shield."

"I already told you, I came in here with a UN inspection team," she insisted. "The Iraqis told us the mine had been abandoned, but our satellites had detected way too much activity in the area. They came back and said their factory at Al-Qaim had been extracting uranium from phosphorus about ten years ago but the project had been cancelled. We decided to come out here at night to see whether an excavation team was working after dark. When the ISIL fighters came after us, my partner left me stranded. I already gave your men all that information."

"Well, maybe I'm not as gullible as the rest of my team. So did they teach martial arts and demolition at that geology school you went to? How is it that you escaped a twelve-man squad of riflemen and trapped their asses alive in that mine?"

"I told them that a thousand times. That rapist tried to make me blow him and I bit his dick off. There was a loose stick of dynamite near the entrance, I saw it when they brought me in.

I scraped a couple of rocks together and got a spark to light the fuse."

"Sounds like a whole bunch of bullshit to me. I agree that your partner probably left you for dead, that's the way those chickenshit Europeans are. As far as you being a UN inspector, I'll believe that when they start showing Porky Pig on raghead TV."

"Th-th-th-th-that's all, folks," she did her best Porky Pig imitation.

"You know, you got some pair on you," Mc Cord chuckled. "It's a damn shame. In a different time and place, you and me."

"Well, I'm already spoken for, but it's the thought that counts."

"Bullshit. There ain't a man who could keep up with you."

"Anvil to Hammer," the CB radio crackled.

"Ten-four, whatcha got?" Mc Cord snatched the microphone.

"We've just crossed the border into Nineveh Province. We're moving due south into Al Anbar Province. There's nowhere they'll be able to go if they're still coming north. Stay alert, if either one of us come across them we'll shove them back into our forces near Haditha."

"Roger that. If they come our way, I'm sending them straight to hell. Hammer out."

"You sound pretty sure of yourself. What if they decide to use those chemical weapons on you?"

"You got some sharp ears on that pretty little head," Mc Cord smirked. "Problem is, how do you get the gas out of them cylinders to make them work? Besides, everyone knows they're worth a hell of a lot more in the cans than out in the air. Wouldn't be worth setting them out just to ambush a twelve-man squad."

"So why do I get the feeling you guys are a lot more than just another twelve-man squad?"

"Just like I said," he grinned at her. "There's a whole lot more to you than you're letting on."

Glenn Frantz felt like he was finally back in the driver's seat. They found him a small hill where he could set up his sniper position. He was about two hundred yards from where Colonel Hussein had his trucks parked behind a ridge with sloping access to the main road. The plan was for him to take out the driver in the lead vehicle. It would give Hussein's convoy enough time to give chase along the road and take them down with rocket fire.

He saw the dust trail as it approached from a half mile, and began adjusting his scope for the kill shot. Only he did a double-take in disbelief before radioing Hussein.

"Hold your fire," Glenn requested. "I got Lieutenant Cantrell on the passenger side. If you open fire you'll kill the Lieutenant. Hold your fire."

"If they move into our position there'll be a firefight and she'll be the first to go anyway," Hussein replied.

"I can put one through the window, and it'll give them time to decide on a countermove. They'll either turn south or backtrack, in either case we can chase them down. Have the Iranians and Captain Shanahan begin their flanking maneuver."

"This is Shanahan. We're in motion."

"Ten-four. I'm putting my men back on the trucks. Proceed. Cobra out."

Glenn took aim and fired, shattering the windshield of the APC as it lumbered along the road. He watched as the vehicle slammed on its brakes, a group of soldiers scurrying from the rear and taking cover behind the truck.

"All right, lady, your time's just about up," Mc Cord reached past Debbie and opened the door before shoving her out. "I need to know what's up on that hill."

"I'd say there's a sniper up there, wouldn't you?" she asked before hitting the dirt with Mc Cord landing on top of her.

"Want me to waste the bitch, Mike?" Qawi crawled over and jammed a pistol in her ear.

"Not just yet. Get Judah and Mugabi around the corner of the truck. That's two on one, we can back that son of a bitch down."

Judah the Israeli and Mugabi the Nigerian were accomplished snipers and were eager to accept the challenge. They quickly assembled their rifles and began peppering the ridge until they detected movement.

"We got the son of a bitch," Judah called over. "He's right there next to that tall boulder. We can pin him down so you can send someone up to get him."

"I'll go," Dundee the Australian offered. "You'll know it's clear when I toss his head off the cliff."

"Hold on," Turnbull the Englishman peered through his binoculars. "We've got company at twelve o'clock."

The squad stared in alarm as Colonel Hussein's trucks began rumbling down the road straight in their direction. They started to climb back into the APC when they saw a dust cloud arriving from the east.

"It's a trap!" Huttig the German bellowed. "They're trying to box us in."

"Anvil to Hammer! Anvil to Hammer!" the CB radio began squawking.

"Hammer to Anvil," Mc Cord reached over the seat and grabbed the mic. "They've got us boxed in. I'm gonna turn around and head back towards Al-Qaim. I need immediate re-inforcement."

"Negative. We're moving in on your nine o'clock. Hold your position."

"What the hell?" Mc Cord was taken aback.

At once there was a dull roar coming from the west, which grew steadily until it began resonating like thunder. Turnbull focused on the crest of the hillside and was jubilant upon seeing a wave of APCs and DPVs heading straight toward their position.

"I think our friends are about to bite off more than they can chew," he grinned.

Colonel Hussein blanched at the sight of thirty vehicles bearing down on him, their M60 machine guns pouring lead in their direction. With six vehicles at his command, they were outnumbered five to one. He ordered his men to take positions behind the trucks as they parked in a defensive horseshoe pattern. He knew it would not hold for long against the enemy RPGs. If routed, they would retreat to the hillcrest where they would make their last stand.

"All right, we need to flank the bastards," William Shanahan ordered as the APC began slowing in its course running parallel to the main road.

"Are you mad?" Shiraz hissed. "I've got two trucks with two M60s. If they get the range on us they'll send us to hell. I'm willing to take up sniper positions further south outside Al-Qaim, but I'm not sending my men to their death out here."

"If you withdraw, Colonel Hussein doesn't stand a chance. Plus you have Lieutenant Frantz stranded on that cliff," William drew his gun and held it in his lap. "You park this son of a bitch and deploy your men or they'll be climbing out of a wreck."

"You're out of your mind, you limey bastard," Shiraz snarled as he pulled the truck over near a slope leading to a marsh. "ISIL takes no prisoners, don't you know? Not to mention the fact they'll sell your woman into whoredom."

"That's the chance she'll have to take. Now get your men out of those trucks and up that hill."

Jessica joined William as they raced along the west side of the hill, Shiraz and his men deploying to the north side. Only the entire unit was forced to the ground as loud, steady thumps precipitated the shower of grassy clumps through the air. The M60s were chewing up the countryside, pinning down the Quds Force so the ISIL fighters could advance to more favorable positions.

"They're going to walk right in here and start tossing grenades at us," Jessica yelled, having raised her AK-47 and nearly having it shot out of her hand. "We're too heavily out-numbered. You need to call Baghdad and request air support."

"You've got to be kidding," William peered out behind a rock, looking for an opening. "Those silly bastards'll drop a load right on our position. We need to find a way off here and draw their fire."

"If we come off their ledge our next stop will be six feet under," Jessica said before a 7.62mm round blasted sand into her face.

Judah chuckled as he peered through the scope of his sniper rifle. The Hammer of Allah squad was in process of pinning down the Iranians while the ISIL battalion was encircling the Kurds. Once this detachment was neutralized, it would be a simple matter to weed out the hijack team and get the chemical weapons back en route to Lebanon.

"There's two up there on that crest," Mugabi nodded to where Judah nearly took out Jessica. "Why don't you let me smoke them while you wait out that lone wolf on that ridge?"

"Shit, I could take that bastard out with a mirror over my shoulder," Judah scoffed before one of Glenn Frantz's bullets caught him right between the eyes.

"FIFH! FIFH!"

The Islamic Force commanders stared to the east as the chant echoed across the field over a set of loudspeakers. At once a great cloud of smoke rolled across the plains, rising in intensity as a wave of purple haze. The guerillas fired a volley of shots into the smoke but were again distracted by Hussein's men as they intensified their own fusillade. The commanders swore and cursed until the ISIL riflemen forced the Kurds to cover with a withering hail of automatic fire.

"FIFH! FIFH!"

The commanders exhorted their men to drive back the smaller force, though one of them spotted something through the corner of his eye. He turned to behold an APC rolling forth from the purple smoke, the speakers blaring the recorded chant from its roof. He angrily grabbed one of his grenadiers aside and took his RPG-7, loading the weapon and readying it for use. He raised it and aimed it at the vehicle as it continued directly toward them, about a hundred yards away.

"FIFH! FIFH!"

The rocket spurted forth and scored a direct hit on the front grille of the APC. It erupted with a great roar, but the secondary and tertiary explosions made him realize something was terribly wrong.

Jack Gawain and Lucretia Carcosa had masterminded the hijacking of the sarin gas delivery. Upon capturing the cylinders, they rigged the truck with explosives to convert the vehicle into a 'dirty bomb'. They set it so that the gas would be projected forward from the truck, and would send the truck into the target zone so that the wind would help propel the fumes. As it turned out, the west wind blew the gas straight into the midst of the Islamic Army forces.

Most of the guerrillas were blinded by the gas, and began stumbling confusedly before the sarin began to suffocate them. Their leaders tried to give orders but began gagging and choking as the gas entered their lungs. Those who breathed deeply of the sarin began losing consciousness, while many fell on the ground and trembled with convulsions. Others had become paralyzed, while many experienced respiratory failure that killed them within minutes.

A number of the fighters had seen the effects of poison gas in Syria and covered their faces as they fled from the fumes. They were almost thirty in number, and as they saw FIFH emerging from the smoke screen, they saw a chance of revenge. They drew their bayonets and machetes, charging at their tormentors who seemed eager for a fight. The Fearless Iranians From Hell drew their weapons and charged into the larger force.

"Come on!" William Shanahan yelled as he led his group of Shiites into the fray from the west, coming in from behind the ISIL fighters. All of a sudden the sides were nearly even. "Let's teach these bastards a lesson!"

Many of the radical Muslims were enraged that women had dared take a hand in a fight against men. As a result, a large number charged at the two females in an effort to chop them down. In response, Lucretia Carcosa and Jessica Anderson stood back-to-back, swirling their blades while bobbing and weaving to avoid the murderous blows. The women were soon covered with blood as their machetes cleaved skulls, severed limbs and ripped torsos asunder. Many who waded into them slipped on the entrails of their comrades before having their arms or legs cut off. Others fell backwards with their heads dangling from their necks. One man walked backwards for ten feet with his head chopped off.

"All right, it's over!" Glenn Frantz called to the girls, who appeared as if someone had dumped a bucket of blood over their heads. They remained back-to-back, waiting for anyone to come close enough for butchering. "Stand down, we've beaten them."

"Jack Gawain, you old rascal," William could not help grinning from ear-to-ear. "How could I not have known you'd be behind this fiendish cleverness?"

"Aye, an' how'd I not figured ye'd come to the resce at th' last minute?" Jack chuckled despite himself. They stared at each other for a long moment before finding themselves in each other's arms.

"I'm Jessica," she wiped the blood from her face before exchanging handshakes.

"I'm Lucretia," she managed to clear the blood from her eyes. "You're pretty good with that thing."

"So are you. I like your style."

"It's not over yet, my friends," Colonel Hussein's DPV rolled up to where the survivors stood amidst a sprawl of corpses. "The main unit took off for the Syrian border. I am quite sure they are the mercenaries. They slipped through the battle as if they were off for a drive through the countryside. There's not many places to hide out there. We'll have them soon enough."

"Let us lead the chase," William insisted. "They'll see a small force and think they're home safe. If they stop to finish us off, you'll be able to take them in short order."

"Well, you'd better get going," Hussein relied. "They've got about fifteen minutes on you."

"I can handle that," Jack nudged William. "Gimme the keys, I'm drivin'."

With that, the two squads rushed to nearby vehicles and prepared for yet another date with death.

Chapter Eight

Mahomet Qawi finally eased the vehicle into the horseshoe canyon outside Deir Hafer that evening. The Hammer of Allah eluded their pursuers over the rocky desert, zipping in and out of wadis, ridges and depressions in making good their escape. By the time they reached their hideout, they were mentally exhausted and looking for rest. They knew the night was far from over as they were scheduled for a debriefing by Mustafa Hilal. The imam was not going to be happy upon learning that the mission had gone horribly wrong.

"What?" Mustafa Hilal exclaimed upon being told of the debacle. He stood with Mc Cord and his mercs in the great throne room over which the Ayatollah presided. "How could such a thing have happened? With all your training, all your preparations, all of our careful planning! These bombs were to be released in Tel Aviv, in Bethlehem, in Jerusalem! They would wreak havoc in New York, in Washington, in London, in Paris!"

"Look, I heard all this before, spare me your bullshit," Mc Cord was irritable. "You need to blame it on them limp dicks who got ripped off for the transport. Me and the boys were right on schedule, even when we got intercepted by them Kurd bastards. Them Islamic Army boys would've made mincemeat outta them Kurds if those hijackers hadn't ran them sarin bombs into us.

You need to point your finger at the clowns who gave up them cylinders."

"Let us not forget that the money promised to all of us by our Saudi financiers is based on performance," Mustafa reminded him.

"Yeah?" Mc Cord got in his face. "Let me tell you that if I'm a dime short on that hundred grand that's supposed to be in my Swiss account, I'll come back here and snap your scrawny neck!"

"Enough of this bickering!" the voice of the Ayatollah bellowed, echoing throughout the chamber. Each of the mercenaries, along with Mustafa, genuflected to remain on one knee with their heads bowed. "Allah is the god of new beginnings, not of lost opportunities! As you quarrel among yourselves, my servants are bringing phosphorus up from the depths from which we will obtain the coveted uranium! We will unleash death and destruction against the infidels across the planet! Your mission is to bring the uranium from Akashat to Lebanon where our allies in Hezbollah will build the dirty bomb we require."

"Sir, my boys and I will be more than glad to bring that uranium wherever you want it. I just cannot accept responsibility for anyone else dropping the ball on this deal. From what I could see, there was a lone squad that sent that truckload of sarin into them Islamic Army boys. If my team had possession of the cylinders, I would've taken them hijackers' heads and set them on pikes on the outskirts of Baghdad."

"You are a good and loyal servant, Mc Cord. Upon the day of your death, you will join me in Paradise where a hundred virgin servant girls await you."

"I'll be looking forward to it, sir."

"It is now time to bring forth the female captive you have taken from the infidels!" the Ayatollah ordered. "It is time to sacrifice her to Allah! We will cut out her heart and slice her into pieces to be sent to the Shiites of Iraq!"

Debbie Cantor remained bound and gagged in a small cell not far from the throne room. She heard the clinking of metal outside and realized her time had come. The door swung open, and she decided that she would struggle to her last breath.

"Take it easy, Deb," she heard Glenn Frantz's voice, and it was the first time she could remember that she felt like crying. "We're going home. It's almost over."

Her bonds were cut loose and the hood taken from her head. She could see there were two other women in the room, and she was handed a machete as they snuck out of the small chamber that had been carved into the cave by Mesopotamians almost six thousand years ago. The air was thin and her legs were wobbly from being cramped up and having little to eat. Yet she found herself galvanized by her rescuers and would fight to gain her freedom.

The tunnel ran in a circle along the second level above the throne room. There were niches cut into the rock wall so one could peer down onto the great chamber below. Platforms were fashioned on opposite sides of the walkway which allowed servants of the palace to bring furniture and fixtures up and down from upper storage areas. Two clerics appeared on the walkway across from Glenn and the others, calling down frantically to their comrades.

"The girl has escaped!" the imams announced. "She is no longer in her cell!"

"That's bullshit!" Mc Cord yelled back. I tied her up and locked her up myself! One of you idiots must have left the cell door open!"

"I can clear th' mystery up fer ye, boyo," the voice of Jack Gawain called out from an alcove to the left of where the Ayatollah sat. "It was I who let 'er by."

"All right, boys, let's finish this!" Mc Cord pulled his machete. Everyone in the chamber knew that ricocheting bullets would bounce around the polished rocks like BBs. This would be a knife fight to the death.

"They're not alone," Captain Malik Shiraz and Lieutenant Farid Gorgan of Quds Force made their presence known as they stepped forth from the shadows to the far left of Gawain and Shanahan.

"You got that right," Glenn and the three female agents raced down the stairs, standing twenty yards to the left of the Iranians.

"Eleven against eight, I like the odds!" Mc Cord grinned wickedly. "Let's take 'em!"

Mc Cord, Dundee, St. Laurent and Turnbull raced towards the alcove where William and Jack stood. The teammates took a flying leap and lunged boots first at the mercenaries. The four men were knocked backwards, both St. Laurent and Turnbull having caught boot heels squarely in the jaw. William and Jack rolled to their feet and drove their machete blades deep into the throats of the fallen men.

"There we go," Jack grinned as Mc Cord and Dundee stared at their dead comrades. "That kinda evens the score, doesn't it?"

Shiraz and Gorgan found themselves pitted against Arkoff, Van Damme and Mugawi. Shiraz screamed out an oath to Allah before charging wildly at Mugawi. The two Muslims drove their blades into each other's bellies to the hilt, and slowly sagged to the marbled floor as the lifeblood spilled out of both men. Gorgan feinted at Van Damme and Arkoff, and all three men slipped on the bloodied floor and fell on their backsides.

Qawi, Huttig, Flores and Guzman began squaring off against Glenn, Lucretia, Debbie and Jessica. Glenn signaled the women to spread to his left as he moved right, drawing Qawi away from the others. The other three mercs smiled confidently, knowing they would make short work of the smaller and weaker females. The women moved back in unison, reaching behind their backs with their right hands while extending their left arms. The men watched as the girls began crouching in defensive postures, and took the opportunity to charge. As they leapt at the women with killing strikes, the three of them threw their left forearms up to block the blades. Each of them had found candlesticks in the upper chambers and tucked them under their sleeves to protect them from hacking blades. In perfect precision as if executing a martial arts form, they drove their blades up into the crotches of their attackers.

Dundee the Australian was a man of great strength, having survived in the Outback since he was a mere child. He locked up with William before hoisting him and slamming him against the marble floor. William lost his blade and tried to defend himself but was swept off the floor and smashed against the wall. At once a great electric shock surged up his spine, and he was in agony as Dundee forced the blade closer to his throat.

"This is the end of the line for ye, mate," Dundee grinned as he was nose-to-nose with William. "The last thing ye'll ever smell is me stinkin' breath."

At once William heard a loud thump as Dundee fell limply in his grip. He stared over the Aussie's shoulder and saw Jessica rushing over to him.

"That's okay, Captain, it's all over. I brought you something," she produced a syringe full of morphine and plunged it into his lower back. "You sit back, I'll get you out of here."

Arkoff had jumped onto the fallen Shiraz and tossed his knife away before proceeding to carve the Iranian's eyes out of his head. Shiraz's screams echoed throughout the chamber as the Russian took great delight in his work. Yet he failed to notice that Shiraz had pulled a stiletto from an ankle sheath before plunging it into Arkoff's back, The Russian drove his blade through Shiraz's windpipe before falling dead to the floor.

Glenn had managed to keep Qawi at bay until the Muslim realized he was cornered by the women who were approaching from behind. He broke into a defensive stance, feinting at the four agents as they awaited his next move. Only Debbie had heard him boasting time and again about all the women he had raped and mutilated, and she was going to give him his due.

"Back up, ladies," Debbie raced forth and slammed him to the ground from behind with a flying tackle. "This one's mine!"

Jack and Mc Cord had slashed and hacked at one another, cutting each other viciously but unable to gain the advantage. Finally Jack found himself at the edge of the dais, with the glaring Ayatollah sitting to his left and Mc Cord crouched warily to his right.

"Well, here we are, a Scots-Irishman standin' here in th' middle o' nowhere, with a Yank and a dick-yankin' Muslim with no place to go," Jack taunted the Ayatollah.

"Fool! All who incur my wrath must die!" the Ayatollah roared. With that, he tossed a great fireball that appeared as a small comet as it zeroed in on Jack. Only he anticipated the move, diving as a great cat to the floor and rolling behind Mc Cord. The fireball slammed into Mc Cord and ignited him like a human torch, the Texan's screams reverberating throughout the room.

Van Damme saw his opportunity, creeping up behind Jessica as she helped William into a sitting position. He grabbed the woman by the hair and brought his blade up to slit her throat. He was entirely unaware of Glenn, who stepped up behind him and fired a bullet into his head.

"No chance of ricochet at this range," Glenn smiled at Jessica.

"Hello!" Lucretia called out, the Black Queen of the Citadel holding Mustafa Hilal by the scruff of the neck as they stood at the platform on the second landing. "I've caught another one."

"Good show, love," Jack called back to her. "Treat 'em right, then, won't ye?"

"Certainly," she said, shoving Hilal headfirst off the platform. He fell screaming to the grade level, his neck breaking as his skull cracked like a melon on the floor.

"It looks like the jig's up, Ayatollah," Glenn called to him as the agents slowly approached the dais. "Come on down quietly, and we'll take you back to Baghdad for justice."

"Fools!" the old man snarled, rising angrily from his throne. "All I need do is gesture…!"

William Shanahan was not sure if he was awake or dreaming. Jessica had dosed him up so heavily that his back felt as good as new. Only it seemed as if he was at the bottom of a goldfish bowl as the great room swirled and swayed before him. He waved his hand before his eyes and it stretched like taffy, his fingers extending a foot long before he made a fist which turned into a shimmering blob. He tried to stand up but his legs turned to jelly, feeling as if he was sitting in a great bowl of chocolate pudding.

He stared in horror as the Ayatollah stepped forth from the throne, his eyes rolling back in their sockets as he swore oaths to Allah unspoken since the days of angels and demons. The agents' smirks soon changed to mouth breathing gapes as they watched a great plume of black smoke rise from the middle of the floor. The hair rose on the napes of their necks as the smoke soon took the form of a rubbery, amorphous mass. They began firing at the monstrous shape to no avail until it assumed the look of a ten-foot-tall black Cyclops from the ancient Mesopotamian legends.

The agents reeled in horror as the Cyclops pulled out a scimitar nearly six feet long and weighing fifty pounds, its blade as sharp as a razor. The monster lifted the blade over his head and drove it with terrifying force into the floor, cleaving the marble as Debbie Cantor barely dove out of the way.

"Spread out!" Jack yelled. "We got t' take 'im separately an' distract 'im, or he'll tear us all t' shreds!"

The monster rose to his full height, allowing Lucretia to leap from the balcony onto his neck. She straddled the beast like a horse, scissoring his neck while holding on to the two-foot horn protruding from its head. He started to raise his scimitar but Glenn chopped at his hand, hacking off its thumb and causing the great blade to fall crashing to the floor. Jack raced up from behind and chopped at his left ankle, severing his tendon in dropping the ogre to its knees.

"Damn it, Luci!" Jack screamed at her. "Get down from there before yer killed!"

At that, the beast reached back and grabbed her by the blouse. She responded by driving her machete into its eye. The monster roared in agony, pulling her off his back and flinging her across the chamber. She landed with a thud on the marble and slid over to where William laid. They tried to speak to each other but were unable to do more than move their lips.

"She blinded it!" Glenn cried out. "We have to take it down!"

Debbie and Jessica made a plan between them. As the monster groped for his fallen weapon and tried to steady himself on his good leg, the woman slid beneath his legs and chopped at his naked testicles. The beast's howls were greater than ever, its frightening pitch piercing their ears as the women rolled away. The Cyclops slipped in his own blood, then slumped in a heap in exhaustion and slowly bled to death.

"That's it, Ayatollah!" Glenn pointed his pistol at the cleric's head. "No more games!"

"Infidel!" the Ayatollah began gesturing again. "I will stand in judgment of your souls in Paradise as you burn in the flames of Hell!"

Suddenly there was a great plume of smoke that enveloped the dais. Glenn emptied his pistol at the throne but the Ayatollah had disappeared into thin air. The team began to regroup, creating a makeshift stretcher with materials found in the upper chamber. With that, they placed William on the pallet and made good their escape.

As William gently rocked on the stretcher while Jack and Glenn toted him out of the mountain stronghold, it was as if he was being spirited away to a far-off time and place. He could feel the desert breeze comforting him as if wafted over his face. Only he detected the scent of sea water, and he opened his eyes to behold a sunny azure sky. At once he realized he was on an ocean cruiser with his head in Morgana's lap.

"Morgana, my darling. I had a terrible dream," he reached up and touched her lovely face.

"You were twitching a bit, but I didn't want to wake you. I love to watch you when you sleep. It makes me think of what our little boy might look like."

"I just…" he started to raise himself up but felt a shock in his back.

"Just rest, darling. Relax. That's what a honeymoon is for."

"Still…on honeymoon."

"We've got two weeks to go, last time I counted," her emerald eyes shone as he reached up and caressed her golden locks. "We finished up the Mediterranean part of the cruise. Next stop is Australia."

"I'll never stop loving you, Morgana. You know that."

"Well, we just got started," she playfully touched his nose. "We'll see if you still love me when I'm old and gray."

"I'll love you more every single day. By that time I won't be able to stand to be away from you for a second."

"Well, good. Hopefully you'll never take another of those missions of yours again."

"No, for god's sakes, no, Morgana," he stared intently into her eyes. "No more. I told them I wanted a desk job, that I wasn't going out again. I meant it. And I don't ever want any secrets between us, for no reason whatsoever. I don't ever want to hide anything from you. You are my soulmate, my other self, my only reason for living. I know that now. I'll never volunteer for anything that will cause me to shield you from the truth."

"My goodness, why so serious?" she ran her fingers through his hair. "What kind of dream did you have? Tell the truth, I wouldn't mind you waking up that passionately more often."

"It was...the kind of dream that makes you realize what's really important in life. You know, I was always the first the volunteer because I knew I could get the job done...better than the next fellow. A lot of it was ego, I'll admit. I was MI6's Gold Standard. I wanted to set the standard for everyone else to follow. Only as time goes by, you realize there's a new challenge every day, and you'll never meet them all. One day you just have to realize that the fellow standing behind you has to get his turn. You just have to learn to let it go. I think I've finally learned."

"I'm happy for you."

"I want a son. I want you to have my son."

"Suppose it's a girl?"

"If she looks like her mother, I'll be doubly blessed."

She placed her hand against his cheek and he kissed her fingers. Only when he closed his eyes he began spinning out of control again...

...and he woke up dreaming.

Chapter Nine

The agents took one of the APCs parked outside the Ayatollah's lair in Deir Hafer, and made a beeline heading east to Al-Qaim. William and Jessica had accomplished their mission in killing Mustafa Hilal and destroying the Hammer of Allah, seriously damaging the Islamic State's mercenary network. Debbie and Glenn completed their assignment in collapsing the uranium mine at Akashat and destroying the sarin bombs recovered from Iraq. Only Jack and Lucretia had not fulfilled the CIA's request in assassinating the Ayatollah Qom Diabolus.

William had suffered a hairline fracture of his vertebrae, and the fight with Dundee had exacerbated the injury. Jessica had some training as a nurse and realized he would need a local anesthetic. The two remaining syringes of morphine would ease the pain but would require them to carry him to and fro. The bouncing of the truck along the road was not helping matters, but the team had no choice but to reach Baghdad before the Islamic Army found out where they were. They had no idea where the Ayatollah was, or whether he had alerted the terrorists. The faster they could move, the better chance of survival they had.

"How far are we?" William slurred, feeling comfortably numb after the last shot.

"It's hard to say. It's a foreign GPS and Glenn's having trouble operating the vehicle as is. We're doing well. Once we cross the

Iraqi border we have as much of a chance of getting spotted by Kurds as the Iraqi Army."

"Aye, boyo, those Kurds did a helluva job gettin' us where we had t' go," Jack tapped his boot as they all sweltered inside the carrier. "Those Shiites are damned lucky they're fightin' on the same side."

"The same could be said about you," William managed. "When I heard reports of FIFH, I thought there was a bunch of madmen running loose in the desert."

"Is that anything new?" Glenn called back.

"Where'd you get that name anyway?" William asked.

"I was into punk and hardcore when I was a ween," Jack replied. "In one o' th' foster homes I was stayin' at, th' older brother used t'play all that stuff. There was a band out o' San Antonio Texas that went by that name. It seemed like a lovely idea t' me."

"The Fearless Iranians From Hell," Debbie smiled and shook her head. "Only in America."

"And I always thought you were so original," Lucretia teased.

"Well, we all can't come up with the Black Queen of the Citadel, now can we?"

"*That* was clever," Jessica said admiringly. "The prisoners we took sounded as if they'd seen a ghost."

"I wish I'd have thought of it," Debbie said wryly. "I might've been able to talk my way out of that mess I got myself into."

"Well, when ye get back t' London, ye let 'em know all th' witnesses ye have t' yer actions above and beyond th' call," Jack told her. "I'm sure they'll give ye one of them trinkets like they gave me an' William th' first time we went out. What was it, boyo, the Distinguished Service Cross?"

"What'd you do with yours?" William grinned drunkenly. "Pawn shop?"

"It seems I gave it t' th' wrong lass, mate," Jack said regretfully.

"Afraid I wouldn't qualify," Debbie said. "I'm Jewish."

"Well, that shouldn't be a problem," Jack quipped. "The National Front hasn't come into power just yet."

"She means we're Israelis," Glenn glanced back over his shoulder. "We're with the Mossad."

"I think you should get a selfie, Jessica," he squeezed his partner's hand. "I'm quite sure it may be the first and last time you'll ever see a Mossad agent on the field."

"If I had thought to bring my phone, I'm quite sure it wouldn't be working very well by now."

"Speaking of souvenirs, I missed the part where you caught up with that rapist Qawi," Lucretia mentioned to Debbie.

"I'd considered keeping his balls for a souvenir, but I didn't have a baggie," Debbie said quietly. "So I just left them in his mouth."

"You go, girl," Lucretia smiled as she and Jessica exchanged fist bumps with Debbie.

"So how is it that O'Shaughnessy didn't tell us you were coming out, Jack?"

"I'm afraid he mightn't have known. We caught a ride with the Yanks, y'see."

"The CIA?" William seemed to come out of his haze momentarily.

"Aye. They were kinda askin' us t'work off a debt."

"It wasn't about that Eiffel Tower affair, I hope."

"You weren't joking, were you?" Jessica was wide-eyed.

"A case of mistaken identity," Jack insisted as everyone, including Glenn, stared incredulously at Lucretia.

"Keep your eye on the road," William suggested. "Now would not be the best time to be given a ticket."

"I don't understand," Debbie could not help herself. "The Black Queen had a nuclear weapon in the Eiffel Tower. It would have blown up women and children."

"The Israeli government is blowing up women and children in Palestine as we speak. Does your cause make it any more justified?"

"You were doing it for money!"

"Your government does it for real estate. Does it make your cause more noble?"

"Deb, we're not here as diplomats, we're here as agents. Let's just play nice and make sure we all get home in one piece," Glenn insisted.

"I, for one, am certainly glad we're on the same side," Jessica looked from William to Jack.

"We've always been on th' same side," Jack pointed at himself and William. "We just got Luci to come on board with th' home team."

"Just out of curiosity, what could have possibly made you so persuasive?" Debbie folded her arms.

"I joined the Citadel," Jack said matter-of-factly. "That made me one of hers. The Spetsnaz commandos who were gonna ship their dirty bomb t'New York tried t' take me out. Luci took the bullet that was meant for me. Ye can thank Luci for savin' New York City."

"That makes her one of the good guys, just like Jack said," Glenn called back. "Isn't that right, Deb? We both got family in New York."

"That's right," Debbie said softly. Luci held up her fist, and Debbie gave her a fist bump.

"How far are we from Al Qaim?" William rasped.

"We're not too far," Glenn replied. "We should be getting close. We'll probably be able to see the mine at Akashat soon."

"I don't know if it's the morphine," William slurred, "but I smell air strike."

The agents simultaneously recognized the gasoline smell as they took turns peering from the hatchway. A 1,000-pound bomb had been dropped in front of the entrance to the mine at Akashat, preventing Islamic Army crews from reopening the mine. The blast dug a crater into the ground, its walls rising seven feet and descending twenty feet into the pit. Smoke and fumes were still swirling around the site, suggesting the strike had occurred just hours earlier.

"I think we should take a look so we can verify the mine's been rendered inoperable," Glenn suggested. "My people'd rest a lot easier."

"Okay, but let's get a move on," Jessica replied. "I'm running out of morphine, and the Captain's going to be in severe pain when it wears off."

"Roger that," Glenn replied, the APC barging forth into the direction of the crater. The powerful vehicle ground its way up the slope and broke through the upper rim of the gorge. It bounded down the slope and began churning its way across the scorched earth.

Just as they reached the other side, they heard the sound of trucks arriving from a distance. The agents climbed out of the APC, scurrying to the east side of the crater in leaving William behind in the truck. He pulled himself together and woozily clambered out, at once taken aback by what he saw.

It was a two-pronged attack, two companies of Islamic Army cadre closing in from either side. William watched four squads of riflemen leapfrogging past one another as they drew closer to the crater. Glenn raced back to the APC, yanking the rocket launcher loose and handing it to Jessica before giving Lucretia the M60 machine gun. He then brought his carrying case out and assembled his sniper rifle before joining the others.

"Any spare grenades, boyo?" Jack trotted over as the others were preparing to fire on the invaders.

"Help me get down there, Jack."

"Nay, fellow. It'll be too much trouble bringin' ye back when they overrun us. Stay up here an' wait until they start comin' over, ye'll help the rest of us make it back inside."

William tossed a bandolier full of grenades to Jack, who rushed back and handed a couple to each defender. This was a fight to the finish. There was no place for them to go.

The ISIL strategy was to tear down the rim of the crater with rocket fire in order to expose the agents' position inside the crater. Each of the squads along the northeast sector fired a rocket, ripping huge chunks of packed earth from the makeshift wall. The agents scrambled for cover as great clods flew through the air along with rocks that could injure or kill. Once the smoke and dust cleared, the guerillas began peppering the apertures as their fire teams crept ever closer.

"There's over two hundred of them out there," Glenn called over as he carefully took out Muslim after Muslim with head shots. Only each one was replaced by two behind him, confident that the agents would run out of ammunition. "We can't hold them off forever."

"If we try to make it up the mountain, we'll be picked off in plain sight," Jessica called back, one of her rockets taking out an enemy truck in the distance. "Perhaps we should just split up and disperse. Hopefully they won't be able to catch each one of us."

"I'll drag William up here, and us guys'll cover th' three of ye," Jack yelled from where he and Lucretia were picking up the front lines of the Islamic wave. "It'll give ye girls enough time t' slip into th' shadows."

"I agree," Lucretia called out during a brief lull. "We can buy Debbie and Jessica enough time to find cover and slip through the foliage at the foot of the mountain."

"I'm not leaving Glenn," Debbie insisted.

"Well, I'll be damned if I go on by myself, so this issue is settled," Jessica caught two ambitious riflemen with a burst of fire as they came to within thirty yards of the crater.

"We're runnin' outta ammo here," Jack called over. "If ye can cover me, I'll go out an' grab a couple of rifles."

"No way," Glenn yelled back. "You'd be a sitting duck. We'll let a couple of them get close, maybe ten yards. We'll take them out and you can try then."

"We can take the truck out and get the rifles," Lucretia decided.

"The truck's our last chance. If we lose the truck we're on foot for sure. Plus William'll be a dead man," Debbie reminded her.

William was about to speak up, but suddenly a distant buzzing noise gave him pause. It grew slowly but steadily in intensity, as if a swarm of locusts were descending on a field of crops. He looked up and saw the skies slowly being clouded by small planes and miniature helicopters, along with other flying objects he had never seen before. They seemed to be coming from the heavens but soon it was obvious they were coming in from the vicinity of Baghdad.

The drones began swooping over the guerillas' forward positions, shining spotlights and strafing their front lines with automatic fire. The riflemen returned fire, causing the small crafts to explode into pieces. Only they were soon replaced with twice as many drones, and eventually the terrorists realized there were far more drones than there were ISIL riflemen. Their commanders were just as baffled, some calling for a retreat while others ordered that they take defensive positions and hold their ground.

"Will ye look at that!" Jack marveled. "They're sendin' out toy airplanes!"

"Keep your head down," Glenn warned. "We have no idea how those things are programmed, and what they're supposed to be doing."

The agents were fascinated as some of the drones sailed directly into the Muslims' APCs, exploding on contact and sending pieces of molten metal flying across the field. Some of the mini-helicopters were setting tiny robots on the ground that made their way onto the field on small treads. Some of the guerillas ran up to kick them over and were shredded by automatic fire from mini-guns inside the machines. The commanders were realizing too late that most of the fatalities were being caused by their men regarding the drones and robots with complete disdain.

"Fools!" the captains yelled at their men. "Take cover! Do not approach those things! They are armed and dangerous!"

"What's the matter, are you afraid?" one guerilla mocked his comrade as he trotted over to a sandbagged position.

"Afraid of toys? Hah!" the Muslim said scornfully before a tiny robot blew the back of his skull off.

Some of the robots were covered with titanium steel, making them resistant to small arms fire. The jihadists found their bullets were more successful in picking off the flying drones, which allowed the ground robots to reach even closer. As the robots began inflicting heavy damage, some of the guerillas began throwing grenades at them. The tactic backfired as the shrapnel, along with the pieces of the destroyed robots, flew through the air and shredded the mujahideen standing nearby.

DO NOT MOVE. PUT DOWN YOUR WEAPON AND PLACE YOUR HANDS BEHIND YOUR HEAD.

William tried to shake the cobwebs out of his head, but the vision remained. There was a cylinder hovering just over his head about three feet away. It had a screen upon which appeared the face of an ugly kid wearing glasses. Below the screen was a metal gun barrel pointed at him.

"You've got to be shitting me," William managed.

I SHIT YOU NOT. DROP YOUR WEAPON. HANDS BEHIND YOUR HEAD.

"Who do you represent?" William did as he was asked.

WE ASK THE QUESTIONS. SPEAK WHEN SPOKEN TO.

"I'll find out who's behind this. And I'll find out who you are."

SILENCE.

"Impudent little bastard."

William remembered years ago, which seemed like a lifetime ago even though he was in this thirties, when he was stopped by the police over a traffic incident. They found his pistol and it took him hours to get out of jail. He hoped that would not be the case here. He seemed to have lost his perspective, somehow forgetting he was standing on an APC in the middle of a crater surrounded by a battalion of dead terrorists.

WILLIAM SHANAHAN, UK RESIDENT, EX-MILITARY, SECURITY CLEARANCE VALID. YOU MAY LOWER YOUR HANDS BUT REMAIN WHERE YOU ARE.

"I need medical assistance. I have a spinal injury and my partner, Lieutenant Anderson, has my medication."

He could feel the morphine wearing off and it was worse than he thought. It felt like he had an electrode wrapped around the base of his spinal cord. He got jammed up worse than he thought when their jeep got hit a few days ago. Fighting it out with Dundee the mercenary was more than his back could handle. No matter how he shifted his weight he could feel a shock coursing up his spine, and he had a bad feeling that he was not going to be able to walk very far.

WHAT MEDICATION ARE YOU CURRENTLY TAKING

"Listen here, I'm not going to stand here and hold a debate with a damned machine, nor with the snotty little bastard running the machine. You have Lieutenant Anderson brought here."

ARE YOU ADDICTED TO DRUGS OR TAKING MEDICATION THAT HAS NOT BEEN PRESCRIBED TO YOU

"I've had enough of this, you little…" William lunged for the drone, which increased its position by another foot from the ground. William lost his footing on the APC and tumbled off the vehicle. When he hit the ground it felt as if he had been hit by an axe.

"William!" Jessica knelt beside him, turning him sideways and sticking another syringe into his back. "Oh my word. Are you okay?"

"I'm the Gold Standard," he repeated over and over. "I can do anything."

"You'll be fine, my darling." All of a sudden Morgana was there with them.

"I knew you'd come for me," he reached up and cupped her cheek until, at once, she turned into Jessica before he plummeted into unconsciousness.

Chapter Ten

William Shanahan was returned to Baghdad, then flown back to England where he had spinal surgery. He had been given a goodly amount of Vicodin and was comfortably numb all the way up to the time he had his surgery. It greatly improved his mood, and he was much more talkative and cordial with those who sat alongside him in his first-class seat throughout the long trip. He reflected on the fact that he had been somewhat self-absorbed throughout his life. As a matter of fact, he had been downright narcissistic, thinking of himself as MI6's Gold Standard. He thought his shite didn't smell because of his exceedingly high personal and moral standards. Jack Gawain certainly changed his perspective as far as that went.

He considered the fact that he had no real friends. All of whom he considered friends were, in reality, war buddies or business associates. If he had bought the farm on this mission, it was highly likely that Morgana would be the only one at his graveside. She would call Fianna Hesher, and maybe Darcy Callahan. Possibly Mark O'Shaughnessy would show up out of a feeling of guilt. Jack might show up on a whim, and probably bring Lucretia with him. Maybe Joe Bieber of the CIA would come if he was in town, heard about it, and could fit it in his schedule. That would be about it. He definitely had to do something about that. He would begin cultivating relationships so more people would show up at his funeral.

He switched on the TV when he boarded the plane, and there was an *Al Jazeera* feature on the continuing conflict in Iraq. It was reported that the Ayatollah Qom Diabolus was planning to make his claim to power any day now. He would proclaim himself the true Caliph of the Islamic State, pointing to his clerical status as well as his accomplishments in having created a mercenary network across the globe and built his own elite unit, the Hammer of Allah. William found it amusing that he failed to mention the creator of the network was dead and the Hammer had been crushed. Nevertheless, it predicted a serious rift between the various factions in the Islamic State which promised greater turbulence in the days ahead.

The Islamic State, for all its deficiencies, had spread from eastern Syria to western Iraq. The Caliph Abu Bakr Al-Baghdadi had declared a global jihad and called all Muslims to take part. It was a rallying cry to all the disenfranchised and marginalized people of the world to commit acts of anarchy and create chaos in the name of Allah. For the adventurous, the paintball enthusiasts, the ultraviolent video gamers, the gangbangers, the career criminals, the psychopaths, or anyone else who always wanted to open fire in a crowded area, this was a dream come true. Make your way to Iraq and we'll make you a star.

One problem was that the President of Syria vowed to destroy the Free Syrian Army, the Islamic State and all terrorists. There could never be a peace treaty or a ceasefire. These were criminals who had to be annihilated. The Prime Minister of Iraq shared the same view. Yet the Prime Minister of Kurdistan, whose region extended throughout northern Syria and northern Iraq, was certain that independence was the only logical solution for the future of the Kurdish people. It seemed as if the leaders of these nations and organizations were resolved that this conflict would go on forever and ever.

Glenn Frantz and Debbie Cantor would go back to Israel, where the fighting between the government and Hamas would never end. The insurgents would fire rockets from Gaza and the West Bank, gleefully anticipating the return fire that guaranteed civilian casualties. The more dead Palestinians, the more of a world outcry against the Jews. It was 21st century anti-Semitism, and as long as there was a threat to the existence of Israel, the longer Glenn and Debbie would fight. The longer they would be ghosts, the phantoms of society. Like William.

When they wheeled him into the operating room, he wasn't sure whether the doctors were as sure of his conscious state as he was. There seemed to have been some complications. He had never taken narcotics before, and there was something about him having taken too much. There was also something about the unbearable pain having raised his blood pressure to a hypertensive state. It was a whole lot of medical doubletalk, and it all boiled down to the fact they were experiencing technical difficulties. William remembered having an out-of-body experience, and he actually enjoyed the privilege of standing alongside the presiding doctor as events transpired.

"Well, Doctor, what's the synopsis?"

"I think it's just another case of the staff being overworked, as usual," the doctor ruffled through the papers on the clipboard near the operating table where William laid. "We had this fellow's military records, though he hasn't been in the military for a few years. His system wasn't prepared for all the morphine he was given before he got here, plus there were all the hypertension issues created by the back injury. We're lucky this didn't develop into a massive heart attack. Our people just didn't have enough information to have seen this coming."

"Well, are you going to be able to get on with the surgery?"

"Now that we have him on the table, I don't see why not. You don't want to have to cut the poor fellow open again, now would you? He is quite a physical specimen. Almost as if carved from wood. We get more than our share of men in excellent condition, but this man is a cut above the rest."

"The Gold Standard, eh?"

"Yes, you could say that, the Gold Standard. It tells you that this man could have made anything of himself. When you consider the kind of discipline it takes to stay in this kind of shape, particularly at the age of thirty-three, it stands to reason he could have persevered in any field he showed an aptitude in. Of course, I suspect he was motivated by a family member, his father, most likely. That's normally the reason why such a man would stay in the military."

"I didn't really know my father, not that well. We weren't particularly close. He was ex-military, and I wanted to make him proud. My mother passed away before I enlisted, and my father died during my first tour of Iraq. I guess I just focused everything into being the best of the best after that."

"This certainly seems like the kind of man who would have signed up for another term. It was a blessing to him that we decided to get out of Iraq. I have no doubt that he would have tried to find a way to go back out. Regardless, he won't be back on the field again after we're done here."

"Why's that?" William sidled closer to the operating table as the doctor walked over to it.

"Well, we're probably going to have to sever some wires down here," the doctor gestured to William's spinal cord. "You see, there's been prior damage but he probably dismissed it as sports injuries. He suffered significant injury over the past year but didn't have it taken care of properly. We can see there were bullet wounds, but of course it wouldn't appear on his service records. I'm betting he was doing some clandestine work for some government agency. I only hope it wasn't the result of illegal activity."

"Oh, no, not me, You can be sure of that."

"At any rate, we'll remove the nerves in this area so he doesn't have to keep coming back or risk getting addicted to painkillers. The downside is that if he reinjures his back, he may not feel any pain until the damage spreads to other areas of the spine. My best suggestion is that he applies for disability retirement. He definitely would qualify and clearly deserves it."

"I just hope Morgana will be able to deal with having me around the house all the time."

"You know, one of the biggest complaints we get from patients like these is what they'll do with all that time on their hands. The workaholics, the lifers, sometimes they fall into depression after retirement for lack of something to do. That's always baffled me. With all the wonderful things there are in this world, why not get a hobby? Or develop a talent they've given up on in pursuit of their career? They should spend a week working with blind children, or kids with terminal cancer. They would be ashamed of being able to throw their gift of life aside so thoughtlessly There are so many who have so little of it left to look forward to."

"You know, I must keep that in mind."

"Nurse?" the doctor turned to the task at hand. "Scalpel."

Jack Gawain and Lucretia Carcosa were brought to the US aircraft carrier George H.W. Bush as it coasted along the North Arabian Sea. They were met there by Bob Probert of the CIA, who had flown from New York to debrief the operatives. The session went on for hours as Jack regaled them with his candid observations, which were recorded on videotape by the increasingly impatient agents.

"Oh, Jack, we'll be here forever if you don't stop with the anecdotes," Lucretia rebuked him at one point.

"Now, darling," Jack assured her, "any story worth telling is worth telling well."

After the session, they were assigned quarters that would allow them to wash and relax before dinner in the officers' mess hall. Probert brought Jack to a highly classified area along the lower decks of the gigantic vessel after they got situated.

"Well, this looks a lot like one of those video halls on Shankill Road, I'd say."

The two men stood on the upper deck of the large chamber which was crowded by computer monitors upon rows on rows of workstations. Nerds with glasses, dressed in white shirts and black ties, bantered back and forth as images were being flashed on a giant screen taking up the entire wall at the front of the room. Every once in a while there was a cry of victory as the nerds gathered around a kiosk before a roving supervisor came over to verify the event.

"This is the control center for the Drone Project," Probert revealed. "Behind every unidentified flying object is a nerd on the bird."

"Well, I'll be," Jack marveled. "How about a walkabout?"

"Actually I wanted to see if you'd like to have a try at one of them."

"No shite? Well, I had a strange childhood, you might say. I didn't get to develop my skills at video games very much. I wouldn't want to bollocks things up, y'know."

"These things are fairly well foolproof. Plus I can have a nerd sit in with you in case you miss a detail or two."

"To hold my hand, then? Well, in that case, I don't see where it'd do much harm."

"Good. C'mon over here, there's a game in progress."

They descended the metal stairwell and walked over to a wide-screen monitor where the technician invited Jack to sit beside him. Probert also pulled up a chair as they beheld a great rally in progress in the ancient city of Babylon, which was being restored by Saddam Hussein. Ayatollah Qom Diabolus had been scheduled to address an outdoor rally of one hundred thousand Sunnis concerning the question of who was the rightful Caliph of the Islamic State.

It was one hundred and ten degrees in the amphitheater where the multitude had gathered. The people were sweltering and those who had brought water gave to their neighbor in compassion. Women and children had been discouraged from attending the gathering, largely out of concern that they would be unable to endure the brutal temperature. Some men forbade their sons to participate, fearful that they would be considered too weak to follow in the ways of Allah.

The black-clad soldiers of the Islamic State adjusted the microphone at the great podium upon the enormous platform that had been erected for the meeting. Behind them hung gigantic black flags of ISIL, along with portraits of the dark-visaged Ayatollah. A great roar arose as the cleric approached the pulpit, then subsided as he rose his hands in prayer to Allah. The people dropped to their knees in reverence, which gave way to fear as the skies suddenly began to grow dark with clouds.

"What manner of man is this, who even the wind and the clouds obey?" they wondered.

"Behold how Allah bestows his power and might upon his humble servant, the fearsome Qom Diabolus!" the Ayatollah bellowed into the microphone as a cold breeze swept over the masses. "I have demonstrated my power in both Syria and Iraq. I have proven to Allah and his followers that only I am fit to hold the position of Caliph of the Islamic State. Yet I must give credit where due to the honorable Abu Bakr Al-Baghdadi for having come before me and straightened the way before me. Indeed, Al-Baghdadi has broadened the path, making my ascent to the Caliphate a smooth and peaceful one. Let all who hear my words praise Allah for the blessing he has provided through his humble servant Al-Baghdadi."

At once they could hear a loud though distant humming, as if a great locust was descending upon the multitude. Many lowered their heads and beat their fists against their chests, frightened that it was yet another manifestation of the Ayatollah's power. Only Diabolus himself questioned what was transpiring, and walked out to the edge of the stage to raise his eyes heavenward. It was then that he laid eyes upon a single propeller-driven flying object, a cylinder slowly descending to a position just above the podium.

"How now, old Diabolus!" the Ayatollah stared in disbelief at the face of Jack Gawain appearing on a screen in the center of the metal machine. "Didn't think ye'd see me so soon after that showdown at yer cave, did ye?"

"Do you dare to intrude upon a meeting of the holy men of Allah?" the cleric demanded. His bodyguards were about to open fire on the flying object but knew that the shots might ricochet, so refrained in awaiting further orders.

"I think that's the least o' yer worries, fellow. Actually I had a different bone I wanted t' pick with ye."

"What?" Diabolus demanded.

"Ye remember that thing yer boys did recently, blowin' up the tomb of the prophet Jonah?"

"And what of it?" the Ayatollah sounded curiously like Jack Gawain.

"Well, here's payback, ye bastard," Jack yelled. With that, the two hundred-pound flying object exploded in a ball of flames. The Ayatollah's bodyguards fell back and watched in shock as Diabolus disintegrated in a cloud of blood. They looked down in awe to see that all that remained of him were his sandals in the very place where he had stood.

The day after surgery, William Shanahan woke up to see Mark O'Shaughnessy and Eric Young standing at his bedside. He was still feeling a bit fuzzy and was genuinely surprised to have his superiors paying him a personal visit in hospital. The MI6 officers, alternately, had that cordial but hurried mien of those who were handling a routine errand before lunchtime.

"That was a hell of a job you did out there, William," Mark said earnestly. "It was perfectly coordinated with our cousins at Langley and our friends in Tel Aviv. Those attacks were all over the telly. Those terrs will certainly take some time to recover. More importantly, you showed the Iraqis what courage and determination can do in the face of superior numbers and firepower. You raised the bar, lad, I can assure you."

"Like Jack Gawain says, 'For God and Country'."

"I daresay that took quite a bizarre twist," Mark smiled curtly. "Can you imagine him and his Black Queen going over the fence, then end up playing on the same side. This is certainly an odd business we're involved in."

"I wouldn't have it any other way."

"It looks like this'll be the crowning achievement of an extraordinary career," Eric noted. "We're going to make sure you get a full pension for disability retirement. Plus there are bonuses and decorations on the table as well. You went above and beyond in going out again for us. Nobody will ever forget it."

"You know how that goes. When you leave Ghost Town, you'll probably never see a ghost again."

"Maybe so, but if you ever need a favor," Mark patted his shoulder.

"They've been waiting to see you," Eric nodded towards the entrance to the private room as the two men took their leave. "We'll see you at the office when you're up and around."

William was genuinely flattered to see Glenn Frantz and Debbie Cantor walking over to his bedside. There was no doubt that they took an extra flight to London for this visit. That meant more to him than any of the medals they would hang on him for this job.

"Looking good, big guy," Glenn smiled, looking more like a college professor in his blue shirt and tie with hound's tooth sport coat. "Last time I saw you, you looked more like an ex-prizefighter."

"Don't be nasty," Debbie slapped his arm, looking like a movie starlet in a black power dress suit and a white chiffon blouse.

"I don't think anyone looked very dignified out there crawling around on all fours."

"I'll tell you, I think I've had enough painkillers for a lifetime," William assured them. "I'm still a little punchy right now, and I can't wait until it wears off."

"Yeah, they took out my appendix when I was in college," Glenn admitted. "I know I never wanted to get doped up like that again. That was definitely a once in a lifetimer."

"You two going to be in town for long?"

"No, we're catching the first flight tomorrow. We just thought we owed it to you to come out and see how you were doing. You and your friends helped save Debbie's life, and you did a big favor for Israel. We'll never forget it."

"All in a day's work. Or was it a week? Damn those painkillers."

"Here's my e-mail address. You keep in touch. If you ever come out to Tel Aviv, I'll show you there's more to Israel than religious tours."

"Maybe if you and Shana find a babysitter," Debbie teased.

"How about you?" William flirted. "Will you show me a good time if I fly all the way out there?"

"Sure," she gave him a big grin. "I'm so looking forward to meeting Mrs. Shanahan."

"I certainly hope you two will take time to see the sights. I'd hate to think you came all the way out here solely on my account."

"Actually we thought we'd kill two birds with one stone," Debbie patted his arm. "We're going to lunch with your friends after they're done visiting with you."

Glenn and Debbie bade farewell before leaving the room to Jack and Lucretia as they came in afterwards. Jack was wearing his bowler hat and black suit, and Lucretia also wore a black hat and dress. One could have easily mistaken them for attending a funeral.

"Aye, well, it's easier to keep black clothing looking clean, don't ye know?"

"So what've you got in mind after this?"

"We're thinkin' of tyin' th' knot, living the easy life like you and Morgana. Y'know, I've pretty well seen everything hangin' with you, boyo. We stopped a couple of nuclear attacks, foiled a plot t' set off a dirty bomb in New York, destroyed ISIL's mercenary network and offed the Ayatollah. I think I've done my share for God and country."

"You certainly have, Jack. I won't forget you. England can never repay you."

"Aye, they could, but they won't. That's why Luci and I have made plans to live off our savings. If ye don't take care of yerself, nobody else will."

"You take care of this fellow, won't you?" William smiled at Lucretia. "He's one of a kind. The world wouldn't be the same without him."

"Nor without you, my friend," Lucretia bent over and kissed his cheek before they exchanged farewells.

"Jack," he called softly, and they turned before they walked out of the room.

"Aye?"

"The Cyclops."

"I wouldn't bring that up again. Someone may think ye mad."

He felt strangely nostalgic after Jack left, a feeling he had long forgotten. It was the worst part about this business, living in a world of shadows. He and Jack had literally saved the lives of millions of people over the last couple of years. Yet no one would ever know about it. Even worse, they might never see each other again. It wasn't the kind of business where you looked forward to getting together with the wives and kids down the road. It was the kind of business where you hoped the past never darkened your doorstep again.

"You look so sad. Is everything okay?"

He looked up and saw Morgana, his angel of light. At that moment he realized she was everything he ever wanted, could ever want. He cursed himself a fool for having ever gotten ill at ease with their relationship, going out and risking his life again like that. He thought of those fairy tales of unfortunates who had traveled the world in search of fame and fortune, and returned in failure to find that there was a treasure hidden in their own back yard.

"Come up here, sit beside me, love," he put the rail down on the side of the bed so she could climb up and cuddle with him. He breathed the fragrance of her hair and decided he could stay there forever and ever, just holding her.

"There's something I need to tell you," she said softly.

"What's that?"

"I'm with child."

At once the tears began flowing from his eyes, as if God Himself had spoken through his friends and his beloved on that morning. His career with MI6 was over, his life as the Gold Standard passed. Everything he held dear was in his arms, right there by his side.

They would live happily ever after.

Dear reader,

We hope you enjoyed reading *Cult of Death*. Please take a moment to leave a review, even if it's a short one. Your opinion is important to us.

Discover more books by John Reinhard Dizon at https://www.nextchapter.pub/authors/john-reinhard-dizon

Want to know when one of our books is free or discounted? Join the newsletter at http://eepurl.com/bqqB3H

Best regards,

John Reinhard Dizon and the Next Chapter Team

You could also like:

Tiara by John Reinhard Dizon

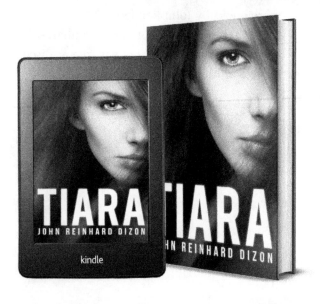

To read the first chapter for free, plese head to:
https://www.nextchapter.pub/books/tiara

CPSIA information can be obtained
at www.ICGtesting.com
Printed in the USA
BVHW041528180121
598054BV00016B/496/J